THE LAST REVENGE

THE LAST REVENGE

It was a simple chore for Vance Jardeen. He had only to go to Camp Sage and process a hundred or so Indians before they could be transferred to a reservation. However, the outbreak of smallpox thwarts his plan. Battling the disease, Vance becomes the target for the settlers' anger over the protection of the Indians. Vance only wants to finish his job and court a young lady but there are other forces at work, and when a ruthless killer strikes, Vance must catch the culprit before he contaminates the entire territory.

THE
LAST REVENGE

by

Terrell L. Bowers

Dales Large Print Books
Long Preston, North Yorkshire,
BD23 4ND, England.

British Library Cataloguing in Publication Data.

Bowers, Terrell L.
    The last revenge.

A catalogue record of this book is
available from the British Library

ISBN   1-84262-468-7 pbk

First published in Great Britain 2005 by Robert Hale Limited

Cover illustration © Boada by arrangement with
Norma Editorial S.A.

Published in Large Print 2006 by arrangement with
Robert Hale Ltd.

Dales Large Print is an imprint of Library Magna Books Ltd.

Printed and bound in Great Britain by
T.J. (International) Ltd., Cornwall, PL28 8RW

CHAPTER ONE

The war party seemed to come from nowhere – everywhere! The attack on the wagon and two outriders was swift and deadly. The warriors shouted and whooped, some shooting rifles and others brandishing tomahawks or lances. They immediately surrounded the small party and stopped the wagon.

Deanna Buckley screamed in terror and grabbed up her six-year-old boy, cradling him to her bosom. The two soldiers on horseback and the wagon driver were cut down before they could defend themselves. Deanna and her son were left to a terrible fate.

Attempting to spare her child, Deanna grabbed for the small .32 caliber pistol from her purse. She would end his life, rather than allow the Indians to kidnap or torture and kill her son.

However, a sudden, sharp jolt sent a searing pain all through her right side. Within an agonizing haze, she realized one of the

Indians had driven his lance into the soft flesh at the base of her shoulder. She lost her grip on the pistol and it fell, useless to the floor of the wagon.

'You die slow, woman!' A sneering Indian spat the words at her. 'You pay for what soldiers do to my people!'

'M-my son...' she gasped, fighting against the agonizing pain of her injury. 'I beg you, don't...'

But the plea died on her lips. An Indian ripped the boy from her arms and he was killed before her eyes. Deanna wailed from the instant heartache and sorrow. She might have been thankful the boy had been spared any suffering, but there was no time. She was dragged down from the wagon and thrown to the ground. A desperate prayer rose to her lips, as several warriors moved in so close they blocked out the sun. She knew she was going to die – a horrible, torment-ing death. Another scream rose to her lips, a final cry of unholy agony.

'No!' Heath Buckley sat upright in his bunk. 'Please! Don't hurt...!'

There came the sound of movement within the room. A match flickered in the dark and the wall lamp came to life. Sergeant Egan was there. He turned up the wick and then rotated to look at Buckley. A sympathetic understanding was etched into his features.

'The nightmare again, Cap?' he asked gently.

Buckley suffered from labored breathing and felt the beads of moisture on his brow. He recovered his composure after a moment and endured a grim embarrassment.

'I didn't mean to wake you, Sergeant.'

His fellow soldier and friend for many years went to the cupboard and removed a bottle and two glasses. He poured a healthy shot into each and moved over to the side of the bed.

'I wish you hadn't been with the patrol that day, Cap,' he said, handing Buckley a glass. 'Bad enough to know those red devils killed your wife in such a cruel manner. You didn't need to see the body.'

'I'm thankful my son didn't suffer.'

'Yes, there's no power or coup to be had by killing an infant. That's something, I guess.'

Buckley took a swig of the liquor. He grimaced at the harsh taste and the burning of his throat as it went down. Unable to conquer the internal ire, his face contorted with hate and malice. 'The worst thing is having those filthy murderers in custody and not being able to get any justice.'

'The War Department has declared the fighting is over,' Egan pointed out. 'If we were to kill Yellow Hand or any of his warriors, it would mean a court martial. I'd wager we would likely end up in a military prison for the rest of our lives.'

'If I knew I could get all of the bloodthirsty savages who were in on the killing of my wife and child, it would be worth it.'

'Yeah, but we don't know which are the guilty Indians. It's possible that Yellow Hand wasn't even along at the time of the raid.'

'They were men under his command!' Buckley sounded off. 'We know Yellow Hand is responsible – whether he was there in person or not!'

'No argument from me on that point,' Egan replied. 'I was only saying what would come up at our court martial.'

Buckley simmered. *Our court martial,* he repeated. 'You say that as if you would walk into that camp with me and help me deal out justice.'

'I've been at your side for a long time, Cap,' Egan said in an off-hand manner. 'I don't reckon I'd let you hang alone.'

Buckley felt a twinge of compassion. It

was rare to experience anything but anti-
pathy and pain since the death of his wife
and child. But Sergeant Egan was as true
and trustworthy as the first ray of sunshine.
He was a man who stood by his word and
would readily give his life for a friend. It was
for that reason Buckley could do nothing.
He couldn't allow Egan to be punished for
an act of revenge. He would have sacrificed
his own life in a minute to settle the score,
but Egan deserved better.

'I'm all right now, Sergeant. I appreciate
your sharing a drink with me.'

Egan offered him a sympathetic smile.
'Maybe, once Yellow Hand and his people
are on a reservation, the dreams will stop.'

'I hope so.'

His friend took away the glasses and set
them next to the cupboard. 'I'll say good
night, Cap,' he said. 'You want the lamp
out?'

'Yes, thank you, Sergeant.'

Egan turned out the lamp and left the
room. Buckley remained sitting up and
listened to the man climb back in to his
bunk. Yes, he was too good a man to end up
in a stockade for helping him carry out his
retribution. If he ever found a way to get
justice for the death of his lovely wife and

son, it would have to be in a manner that did not implicate himself or Egan.

Vance Jardeen had been looking forward to an overnight stop in the town of Deadwood, located in the Dakota territories, thirty-some miles east of the Wyoming border. However, his plan was dashed at spying a crudely written sign, tacked on to a skeletal, leafless tree. It read:

SMALLPOX
No one allowed to enter or
leave Deadwood.

Vance felt as if an icy blast of wind had hit him flush in the face. He was all too familiar with the infectious, death-welding sickness. A decade had passed since the terrible pestilence had beset his home town. It had snuffed out the lives of half the population – his mother and two sisters included.

His father had survived, but was badly scarred and never fully recovered from the loss of most of his family. He died a couple years later, a mere shadow of his former self. Vance had been lucky. He survived with only a few small pockmarks. However, the scars of the gruesome experience were more internal than external. Even though he'd been strong and full of energy at thirteen, the disease had nearly killed him. The deadly disease was something he never wanted to see again.

A rider must have been keeping watch of the main trail. He rode forward and stopped in the middle of the road, fifty feet away. He had a shotgun positioned on his hip and a badge was visible on his vest.

'You read the sign, fellow?' he asked.

'I did,' Vance replied. 'Looks like you've got a snoot full of trouble.'

'Half of the people in town are down sick. We've had eleven deaths to this point.'

'I've had smallpox myself,' Vance said. 'I know how bad it can get.'

'You best ride around Deadwood, all the same,' the man warned. 'If you come into town, you'll be stuck for the duration.'

Vance gave his head a negative shake. 'I only figured to spend a single night. I'm in no hurry to be tied up for a month.'

'I reckon it'll last that long – maybe more,' the lawman agreed.

Vance gave him a sympathetic nod. 'Sorry you folks are in such a fix. I hadn't heard about the outbreak.'

'It come on us a few days back. Soon as we

13

recognized the plague for what it was, we shut down our borders and sent word to the nearby towns by telegraph.'

'Good thinking. With any luck, maybe you can contain it right here.'

'All of our efforts might be a waste of time. A wagon train came through a short while back, just about the time the disease appeared. I'm for thinking those folks were exposed to the pox.'

'I'll watch for them,' Vance promised. 'If I catch up, maybe I can warn them to stay away from any settlements until the danger has passed.'

The lawman bobbed his head up and down. 'I'd appreciate your doing just that.'

'Well, good luck to you, Deputy. I know you'll be needing it.'

The man raised a hand in farewell and Vance turned his horse toward a winding nearby trail. Deadwood was situated at a mountainous base, so the route up the steep side of the hill was the only way to bypass the town.

As Vance rode away, he grit his teeth. The deputy had an unenviable task, watching over a town that was ravaged by smallpox. The lawman had to keep outsiders away, while, more important, he had to keep the present inhabitants from leaving, so they wouldn't spread the wretched disease to other towns. Therein was the hardest part of his duty. When news of smallpox spread through a town, panic usually set in. Those who were not yet showing signs of the disease would try to run, thinking they could escape the dreadful plague. The problem was, they often left too late, *after* being exposed. Not only did they fall victim to smallpox, they ended up spreading it to another unsuspecting town.

Vance rode through the brush and skirted the row of buildings. It was like sneaking past a graveyard at midnight and feeling the presence of the dead. A shroud of doom blanketed the town and a dreadful silence hung in the air. He could think of no place on earth more terrifying than a town infested with smallpox. The pestilence struck down the strong and the weak, the old and even the children. It was an indiscriminate killer and many people died to slake its terrible hunger for human life.

Vance shuddered from a prickling sensation. He had heard it said that a person couldn't get smallpox twice. Even so, he wasted no time putting the town and the plague behind him.

CHAPTER TWO

Captain Buckley looked at the communiqué, then raised his eyes to frown at the corporal.

'Smallpox?' he asked. 'Am I reading this right? There's been an outbreak of smallpox?'

'The telegram is from Deadwood, over in the Dakotas, Captain,' the soldier replied. 'Colonel Voight says you are to see that the disease doesn't spread further west. His orders are for you to use every man at your disposal and patrol every possible route that leads into Wyoming. Every traveler is to be stopped and held in quarantine until there is no chance they have the disease.'

'Do we know how long a period that is?' Buckley asked.

'The post surgeon says no less than three weeks.'

'How did the colonel suggest we confine the travelers – separately or all together?'

'However they arrive. He said we should get a supply wagon and be ready to deliver

16

provisions to those who hadn't expected a three-week delay.'

'And how are we supposed to do all of these things, without putting our own men at risk?'

'The post surgeon checked the medical records. Me and six other men on the post have already had smallpox. We are to be the only ones who make physical contact with any travelers. The colonel said we are to take every precaution to prevent the epidemic from spreading to the post or nearby settlements.'

'What about Yellow Hand and his braves?' Captain Buckley asked. 'If I'm busy guarding the border, who is going to keep that savage and his band of bloodthirsty warriors confined at Camp Sage?'

The corporal replied: 'You are to detail a squad to keep the Indians under surveillance.'

Buckley grunted his contempt. 'A squad!' he snarled. 'A squad isn't enough men to keep an eye on that many Indians.'

'I'm only repeating the colonel's orders, Captain.'

Buckley did some quick thinking. 'All right, Corporal. I'll figure a way to protect our borders and make sure Yellow Hand and his braves stay put until troops arrive to move him to the reservation.' Then his face grew taut and he clenched his teeth in anger. 'I sometimes think the good colonel forgets about Yellow Hand being as dangerous as any disease. He would like nothing more than a chance to escape with his warriors and butcher more white settlers.'

'It is a challenge, Captain,' responded the corporal. 'However, the colonel was very specific about this smallpox outbreak taking precedence. He wants sentries posted and patrols operating within the hour. He specifically stated, it is your responsibility to see that smallpox does not spread into Wyoming or to any point west of here.'

'I will carry out the order,' the captain said tightly. 'Thank you, Corporal.'

The young trooper saluted, turned about and left the room.

Buckley remained at his desk. He watched him make his exit, while fuming with a severe inner rage. Sergeant Egan, who had been waiting outside, entered the room. One look at Buckley's face told him the news had not been good.

'Trouble, Cap?' Egan asked.

'We're to send out patrols and guard the Wyoming borders!' Buckley growled the words. 'The colonel expects me to use the bulk of our troops for the chore.'

'Then the rumor is true – smallpox has broken out in Deadwood,' Egan said.

'That's correct, Sergeant. And I've been appointed the guardian for the rest of the western world.'

'What about Yellow Hand and his people?'

Buckley grunted his disgust. 'We're to have a squad watch over him and his tribe.'

'A single squad?' Egan matched Buckley's contempt. 'If those red devils get to feeling their oats, they could slip away and scatter all over the country. We'll be too busy with the smallpox detail to even catch them.'

'Yes, it's an invitation for those murdering savages to escape and go on another killing rampage!' Buckley pounded his fist on the desk. 'Damn the ignorance of those officials at the War Department! They are crazy if they think Yellow Hand is going to stay on a reservation. You can't teach a war chief and his braves a new way of life. They don't want to give up the old way. They will never change or adapt to a peaceful way of life. The only thing left is extinction!'

'There's getting to be too many bleeding hearts in Washington.' Egan agreed with Buckley's position. 'You can bet, if Yellow

Hand's band of murdering assassins had attacked and killed the families of senators or congressmen, they would have a different point of view.'

'Well, there's nothing we can do at the moment but follow orders,' the captain said, squelching his fury. 'Have the bugler sound assembly.'

Egan ran to obey, but Buckley didn't see him go. Through his hate-clouded vision, the only thing he could see was the pompous sneer on the face of Yellow Hand. The Indian had led a charmed life, always quick to gain the protection of his camp, never being caught out with his warriors. For many months, his men had sneaked out to steal and kill on their raids, then hurried back to the safety of Camp Sage. To Yellow Hand, this exercise in containment was a perverse game.

Buckley swore under his breath. If only there were a way to put an end to Yellow Hand and his murdering followers. He had escaped punishment by playing a deadly game of hide and seek. Once the agent from the War Department arrived, the Indians would be forever protected. That notion caused a burning in his gut, as if he had swallowed a mouthful of molten lava.

'Captain?' The corporal entered the office for the second time and intruded into his dismal thoughts.

'Yes? what is it?' Buckley asked, returning his attention to the present situation.

'A follow-up telegraph message arrived from Deadwood a few minutes ago. It seems a wagon train passed through there, right before they suffered the outbreak of smallpox. They were headed for Salt Lake and are probably coming this way. It sounds as if they were exposed to the disease.'

'Thank you, Corporal. I'll inform the patrols and we'll intercept them as soon as they cross the border.'

The young man gave a quick nod and hurried out of the room. Buckley did not miss the worry or concern in the young man's eyes. Even the mention of smallpox frightened most people.

The bugle sounded and men scurried about, falling into place. Captain Buckley stepped outside headquarters and watched. He thought about the six men who had previously had smallpox. His long-time friend, Sergeant Egan, was one of their number. He would put him in charge and hope this plague passed quickly, without spreading to the post or nearby towns. A man bound by duty, he resigned himself to the chore ahead and took his place at the front of the assembly.

Vance Jardeen spotted the lone wagon. There was no team visible, no sign of life, only a solitary wagon sitting in an open stretch of ground surrounded by rolling hills. It was off the main trail by a hundred yards and appeared deserted.

Curious, Vance guided his mount in that direction. As he approached he could see nothing broken, no axle or wheel damaged, nothing wrong with the wagon itself.

Abruptly, a head poked out from the back of the wagon and an elderly man waved his arms.

'Stay away!' he called out in a hoarse voice. 'We've got smallpox here!'

Vance continued forward, riding up to the rear of the wagon. When he had stopped his horse he could see the old gent was in a bad way. His exposed arms and face were covered with smallpox pustules and his eyes looked like two dark, hollowed-out sockets.

'Stay back, you young fool!' the man rasped, his voice barely more than a whisper. 'Didn't you hear me? We've got smallpox – the plague!'

Vance leaned to one side and looked into the back of the prairie schooner. The stench of the disease assailed his nostrils, and he grimaced at the sight of another pair of bodies lying together.

'How many are you, old-timer?'

'Th-three,' he stammered. 'My wife and I and our niece, all from Kansas.'

'Do you have any water?' Vance asked.

'Not since yesterday morning.'

'Fluids are important in the fight against smallpox,' Vance told him. 'It's the dehydration that kills a good many people.'

'It's too late for the three of us,' the old man said. 'We're about done in.'

'There's a stream back a mile or so from here,' Vance told him. 'I'll ride back and get you some water.'

'God knows you're trying to do the right thing, sonny,' the old-timer wheezed. 'But do you really want to catch this wretched disease?'

'I had it when I was a youngster, old-timer. They say you can't get it a second time.'

The old man continued to squint at him. 'And you're willing to bet your life on it, are you?'

'Without water, you folks don't have a chance to beat this,' Vance replied.

23

'I'm obliged to you.' The man spoke softly. Then he sat back, closed his eyes and slipped into a fitful sleep.

Vance hated to be near the disease that had nearly killed him. But these people needed help.

It took only a glance to know all three of those in the wagon were in the later stages of the disease. They would soon reach the turning point. Either they would die or they would begin a slow, agonizing recovery.

Vance took one of their water barrels to the creek and returned a short time later. He tethered his horse where the gelding could feed on the local wild grass. The weather looked clear, so he threw up a lean-to on the leeward side of the wagon. It was too crowded to treat all three in the back of the wagon so he made beds for the elderly couple under the lean-to.

Carefully, Vance moved the old fellow and his wife to the new beds. He left the younger lady in the back of the wagon and went to work.

With them ensconced in their beds, he began trying to get each of them to take a little water or broth. It was no easy chore, as the fever and torment of the illness had caused the victims to become delirious.

Vance was amazed the man had been lucid enough to speak to him upon his arrival.

About midnight, he took a break from his efforts and sagged down on to his own bedroll to eat his meal. It had been a long while since he had suffered the bout of smallpox. He should have been able to stand the nightmare. But the gruesome killer left deep scars, emotional fears that did not heal. Seeing the devastation up close once more, he had to fight down the impulse to run, to get away from the horrible, lingering death. The pus, the scabs, the smell – it was a grave reminder of when he had lost most of his family and suffered with the terrible misery himself. He was repulsed by the disease, but he knew that, without his help, all three of these people would die.

He sighed resignedly. There was a good chance he was wasting his time. All three of his patients were in dire condition. It was likely the only good he was going to do for them was to provide them with a decent burial.

Corporal Dowd rode up to within a few feet of where Captain Buckley sat his own mount. From the somber look on his face, Buckley knew the news was not good.

'Yonder is the wagon train which passed through Deadwood, Captain,' he said thickly. 'They sure enough have smallpox among them. A good many are down sick.'

'How many cases?' Captain Buckley asked.

'Difficult to say. There are twelve wagons and about fifty people. The man on the lead wagon said about half were infected or had fever. I think it's probably worse than that. From where I sat, I didn't see but maybe two healthy bodies in the whole group.'

'Where did they think they could go?'

'Desperation kept them moving, Captain. I'd say they were hoping to find help.'

'More likely spread the contagion all over the country,' Buckley replied. 'We'll hold them where they are.'

'Sounds like the only option available,' the corporal agreed.

'Sergeant Egan will oversee the situation, but you will take charge of the volunteers,' Buckley ordered. 'Form the wagons in a circle and separate the stock from the camp. I'll see that a wagon with water and supplies are brought to you.'

'You know that once me and the others go in among those victims, we can't come back, unless we change clothes and bathe from

26

head to foot.'

'We'll construct a cleaning station a short way from the wagons. Whenever you men leave the train, you'll have to wash and change clothes.'

'Yes, sir, Captain. What about any other travelers who come our way?'

'Sergeant Egan will keep himself available to interview anyone we stop who is coming from the East.'

'Good enough, sir,' the corporal replied.

'Handle the situation with extreme care,' Buckley warned the corporal. 'We don't want this dreadful plague to spread any further.'

'Understood, Captain.'

'I'll also have a burial detail dig a single pit. Inform the people from the wagon train that we have no choice but to burn the bodies of the dead. They are free to construct individual crosses for each, but we can't chance an animal digging up a body and spreading the disease.'

The corporal displayed a pained expression at the news. 'I'll tell them.'

'Once the ordeal is completed, we'll have to wash down and disinfect the animals from the wagon train. Then every person who survives will need to have a comprehensive bath and fresh clothing. Everything they own must be decontaminated after the plague has passed – money, clothes, wagons, everything.'

'I understand, Captain.'

'Get on back there and take charge.'

'Yes, sir. I'll circle the wagons, get the people settled and make a list as to anything we might need.'

'Good luck, Corporal.'

As the young cavalryman rode back toward the wagons, Sergeant Egan eased his horse up alongside the captain.

'Glad you got me out of that duty, Cap. I didn't enjoy the idea of being a nursemaid to a bunch of sick pilgrims.'

'For the time being you will be the liaison between us and the assigned detail. If we detain any other travelers, you will be the only one to have personal contact with them until they have completed their quarantine.'

'I understand, Cap.' Egan looked at him. 'You got anything else in mind?'

'Maybe,' Buckley said, displaying a thoughtful expression. 'A wise officer can sometimes turn defeat or tragedy into his own victory. There might be a way we can salvage something positive out of this epidemic.'

'Something positive? From a smallpox

epidemic, Cap?'

'It's an idea which has been rattling around in my head. I haven't sorted out any of the details yet.' He straightened his shoulders, returning to the business at hand. 'For the time being, keep a close check on the other patrols.'

'The patrols have been ordered to hold any travelers at bay until I or Corporal Dowd arrive, Cap.'

As the sergeant rode off, Buckley rubbed his chin thoughtfully. He felt a commiseration for the plight of the people from the wagon train. He regretted the idea of having to burn their dead and watching them suffer, for he was all too aware of how much it hurt to bury someone you loved.

Sitting his horse, staring out into space, he shook off the anguish. After every storm, the world grew light once more. With a little luck and plotting, he might glean a ray of sunshine from all the surrounding gloom.

Vance wiped his brow and grit his teeth at the hopelessness of the situation. It was discouraging work, trying to force the three sick people to take sips of water or broth and keep them as comfortable as possible. He didn't get a moment's rest until after

29

midnight. Then he took time to have a cup of coffee and eat a plate of beans.

As he wearily forced himself to swallow each bite of food, he considered his trio of patients. They were a sorry lot. Having all been struck down at the same time, they had been unable to look after one another.

The old couple were in the worst shape, because of their advanced years. The young lady appeared to be a little stronger, but Vance doubted any of the three had more than a fifty-fifty chance. The old man was the worst and probably wouldn't survive the night. As for his wife, she had never become conscious. They were both bleeding at the mouth and were covered with severe blisters. The young woman had seemed aware of his presence, when he treated her, but the agony of the fever kept her delirious.

After Vance finished his meager supper, he went to each of his patients and once again tried to get them to take a few sips of water. However, the Grim Reaper had come forth to take control. The two elderly victims could no longer swallow. The water either caused them to choke or trickled back out of the side of their mouths.

With a heavy heart, Vance took his cup of water and climbed into the wagon. The feeling of helplessness caused tears to burn at the back of his eyes. He had arrived too late to help. The family had already become weak and dehydrated from lack of water or food. He was probably going to lose them all.

He dismissed the blighted hope and turned his attention to the youngest victim. Even as he crawled up closer to her side, a soft moan escaped her lips. He froze for a moment and studied her dark outline. Surprisingly, he saw the girl's eyes blink and open. She rolled her head back and forth from her misery, but appeared to be alert.

Vance forced a smile to his lips.

'Hey there!' he whispered softly. 'Are you awake?'

'Who...' She was unable to speak.

Quickly placing the tin cup to her lips, he waited for her to take a couple sips of water. She closed her eyes for a few seconds, as if to summon her strength. With the flicker of light from his camp-fire, he was able to make out her features more distinctly. When she again opened her eyes, there was a rational spark to her gaze which gave Vance a ray of hope.

'W-who are you?' she asked.

'I'm the neighborhood doctor, ma'am,' he

tried to respond cheerfully. 'I was making a house call on a woodchuck with a tooth-ache, when I happened across you and your family.'

She didn't try to smile. 'My uncle and aunt? Are they...?'

'Still hanging on,' he answered solemnly. 'That's about all anyone can do against smallpox.'

'Aren't you afraid of being so close to us?' she asked.

'I had the disease as a kid, ma'am,' he explained. 'Once you beat it, you're supposed to be immune.'

'The other wagons left us behind,' she explained. 'They even took our team of horses so we couldn't follow.'

'Pretty foolish of them to think they could run away from a disease like smallpox,' Vance said.

'There was a sick person in the last town we passed through. The man collapsed on the main street of town. My uncle and another couple from our train helped carry him to a bed. We all thought he had suffered too much heat.'

'The whole town is in quarantine now,' Vance informed her.

'We spent several days in town, picking up

supplies and readying the teams for the long haul over to Salt Lake City. I fear the entire train is infected.'

'It's likely a dozen people from your group contracted the disease by the time your wagons started rolling. I imagine the rest of your comrades are sitting a few miles up the trail and struggling to get through this epidemic right now.'

'And you? Where did you come from?' she asked.

'I work for the government. I was on my way to Camp Sage. They have a tribe of Indians there, waiting to be processed and settled on a reservation.'

The woman sighed. 'You're a saint for stopping to care for us. My name is Stormy, Stormy Malone – a rather befitting first name for my journey to this point, don't you think?'

'Yes, it would seem your journey has had a *stormy* beginning,' Vance agreed. 'I'm Vance Jardeen.'

'I'm pleased...' she faltered, consumed by fever and pain. She moaned softly from the agony, but still gathered enough strength to finish. 'I'm pleased to meet you, Mr Jardeen.'

'Same here, ma'am,' he replied, 'but I sure

33

would have preferred different circum-
stances.'

She closed her eyes and he thought she
had slipped into unconsciousness. But then
she mustered up the strength to speak again.

'The wagon train was made up mostly of
Mormon families,' she explained. 'They
were on their way to Zion, to Utah.'

'I've heard some refer to Salt Lake City as
Zion on occasion.'

'There are a number of men there who
need wives,' she illustrated. 'My uncle
thought it would be exciting for me to make
the trip with them. I never thought...'

She couldn't finish. Vance tried to take her
mind off of her severely ill relatives.

'You mean to tell me you're of a mind to
maybe end up being married to a man who
already has several wives?'

'No, never that!' she declared with some
force to her words. 'There's a great mis-
giving about the Mormons. Very few of their
men have more than one wife. Besides
which, both the Church and territorial
government have abolished polygamy.'

'For myself, I always figured it would be
hard enough to manage the needs and welfare of one woman,' said Vance. 'I can't
imagine trying to handle more.'

34

'We had such high hopes for a new life in Utah. Now...' Tears seeped from the corners of her eyes, 'now we won't ever get there.'

Vance sympathized with her plight. 'It was rotten luck, arriving at Deadwood when an epidemic was about to break out.'

'My family has had their share of bad luck,' she lamented. 'Drought, locusts, burning sun, and freezing winters. I was desperate to get away from our farm and start a new life. Both of my parents died from the hard work and I ended up living with my elder brother and his wife. When my aunt and uncle offered to take me with them, I jumped at the chance. It was to be a joyous journey.'

'Life has a way of sometimes playing a dirty trick on a person,' Vance said.

'Yes,' she agreed. 'I wish...' But she couldn't finish.

Vance gave the girl a couple more sips of water. This time, it took most of her strength just to swallow. He waited for her to speak again, but she was too exhausted to reopen her eyes.

'You're going to really start suffering from the blisters in a day or so.' He issued a warning as to what lay ahead. 'When you reach the critical point and the itching starts, I'll

35

need to tie your hands. It's for your own good, so you won't scratch or pick at the scabs and cause a lot of scarring.'

'I understand,' she murmured.

'You need to keep your spirits up,' he encouraged her. 'Don't for one moment think you can't beat this. I'm living proof a person can survive smallpox. You just get tough and fight.'

'What about my aunt and uncle?' she wanted to know. 'Are they ... are they both going to die?'

Vance didn't wish to lie to her. 'They are both pretty badly off, and being on the older side, it's too early to tell. I didn't have much luck getting them to take the water and broth. I don't know if they will pull through or not.'

She rolled her head in her agony. Sick and miserable as she was, the thought of maybe losing her relatives appeared to hurt more.

Vance stayed at her side a few more minutes, until she slipped into a fitful sleep. Weary from the long hours, he returned to check on the elderly couple. One look was all it took – his fears had come to pass. The old man had given up the ghost and was dead. The woman lying next to him was barely hanging on and probably wouldn't make it to morning. If he had arrived sooner, he might have been more help to the three victims. As it stood, there was a strong possibility all three would perish.

CHAPTER THREE

Captain Buckley faced the four ranchers with a cool deliberation. They were grim, determined, armed, and primed for a fight.

'I don't want any trouble with you men,' Buckley said carefully. 'But, rest assured, the army is not intimidated by threats.'

'It is the rumor of smallpox which be our concern, Captain.' The man known as Big Irish spoke up. 'That mortal plague can reek holy hell on a town or populace in a very short while.'

'My orders are quite precise,' Buckley answered. 'No one is to enter or leave this part of Wyoming until the smallpox epidemic is under control.'

'We're not of a mind to ride over to Deadwood and give the disease a free shot at us,' Big Irish replied. 'It be the truth of the matter, we're concerned the contamination won't enter this part of the country either.'

'Then we are in agreement,' Buckley said.

'To that end, we aim to make certain that everything is being done to prevent the spread of the disease, soldier boy. We don't intend no one should enter this part of the country till the plague has run its course.'

'I already explained my orders,' Buckley replied. 'We will halt anyone coming from the Dakotas for a three-week quarantine. Once we are assured they do not carry the disease, we will allow them to continue on their way.'

'And what about them Injuns?' one of the others spoke up. 'They've been camped outside of Fort Sage for several months. Our womenfolk are fearful some of them bloodthirsty savages will sneak away in the night and slit our throats!'

'I have their entire camp under armed guard,' Buckley told them. 'None of Yellow Hand's warriors is going to escape the confines of the camp.'

Big Irish gave a nod of his head. 'If even one of them red devils breaks out, we'll be a-taking this into our own hands. We been fighting Indian wars for too many years. It's time this was settled.'

'I can assure you men, I've no great fondness for the Indians either,' Buckley replied. 'But I have my orders and will carry them out.'

'You just make sure them red devils don't

39

escape and start killing, that's what we're saying!'

'If it becomes necessary, we have a stock-pile of barbed wire at the fort,' Buckley advised the four men. 'If we don't get the order to move those people in the next few days, I intend to have a wire fence built around their entire camp.'

'Aye, that much precaution would allow me and my family to sleep a wee bit better at nights,' Irish said.

'Me too,' another man agreed.

'It is an option we may exercise,' Buckley said. 'We are taking no chances with the red devils.'

'We'll be keeping an eye on you soldier boys.' Irish spoke again. 'You be doing a real good job and get rid of them savages forthwith.'

'The sooner, the better, as far as I'm concerned,' Buckley told him.

Irish gave a bob of his head, then he and the others turned around and headed toward the small town of Wayward, Wyoming.

Vance stood over the grave. He had dug it deep, for he couldn't risk having some varmint root the body out of a shallow hole and maybe spread the disease.

He looked toward the wagon. The old woman had made it through the night, but she was extremely weak. It was likely only a matter of time for her. As for the lady in the wagon, she was consumed by delirium, no longer aware of her surroundings. She was at the crisis period, where she would either battle through or surrender to the cursed pestilence.

After saying a short prayer over the grave, Vance checked his patients again. There was nothing more he could do for either of them, so he decided to lie down for a few minutes and try to get a little rest.

Sleep should have come from sheer exhaustion, but it didn't. Vance wondered what the woman would do if she managed to beat the smallpox. His single horse could not pull the wagon, so most of her personal belongings would have to be left behind. They would have to ride double and she would have little more than the clothes on her back! How would she complete her journey to Salt Lake all alone? How would she earn a living?

Vance tried to push the questions out of his mind. People always found a way. If the woman survived, she would find a way. There would be a job of some kind, enough to earn her own board and room. She would make do. The first chore at hand was to survive the deadly disease. Considering her present condition, that seemed a Herculean task.

For himself, he had an assignment to complete. This extended delay was not good. He needed to get off a telegram to the War Department and assure them he was still on the job. As soon as it was possible to travel, he would make haste for the nearest town with a telegraph office.

Sergeant Egan rode up next to Captain Buckley. He wore fresh clothes, for his other uniform had been left at the exchange point, where it would be laundered and disinfected. Buckley waited for him to give his report.

'They are in sad shape over at the wagon train, Cap,' he began. 'Nearly every man, woman and child is down sick. I suspect about half of their number won't survive.'

'How are our men holding up?' the captain asked.

'There isn't a lot we can do but offer the sick a drink of water and support those who are caring for their own.'

'Once all of the animals are driven to a

holding pen, I want them washed down with lye soap and then scrubbed with alcohol. No one is to have any additional contact with them for three weeks. We're taking no chances with the smallpox.'

'It might take a few days, but I'll see it gets done,' Egan said.

Buckley frowned in deep thought for a moment.

'When you get the chance, I have one other chore for you.'

'What's that, Cap?'

The captain handed a folded piece of paper to his sergeant.

'This ought to explain it.'

Egan looked at the order and raised his brows.

'You think this is a good idea?'

'The army's purpose here is to protect the settlers,' replied Buckley. 'I met with a few of the locals recently who voiced their opinion. They are still concerned about a few renegades slipping away and butchering them in the night.'

The sergeant bobbed his head in agreement.

'I understand, Cap. I'll see to it.'

'One other thing,' said Buckley. 'The Bureau of Indian Affairs is sending a man to

43

process Yellow Hand and his band of murderers. I think we should get word to Big Irish and some of his friends. He might be able to help us – how should I put it? – stall the processing for a few days.'

Egan picked up on his train of thought.

'I see your strategy, Cap. I'll slip into town and have a little talk with him. Soon as I've finished with the errand, I'll see about this other little chore.'

'Very good, Sergeant. Once the disease has run its course, the survivors will have to have everything they owned cleaned and disinfected. We take no chances with this.'

'Right you are, Cap.'

'Let me know if you need any supplies. The army stands ready to provide adequate provisions for the people at the wagon train.'

'What are the orders concerning the dead?'

'The victim's remains will have to be burned, to prevent any possible spread by animals digging up a grave. I know it's going to be hard on those people, but it's the only way to have a safe burial.'

'I understand, Cap.'

Buckley grunted. 'How about you, Sergeant? How are you holding up?'

'I'm feeling the strain and I've nearly removed a layer of skin. I never was one to take more than one bath a week. This washing two or three times a day – I feel about as wrung out as an old wash cloth from all the scrubbing.'

'Only way to prevent any chance of spreading the disease to the rest of the men. Be glad we're close enough for you to walk to the wagon train. Otherwise, you'd have to scrub down your horse as well.'

'It's good we are being careful with the plague, Cap. I've got some horrid memories and the pockmarks to prove that this here disease is no fun.'

'I'll take your word for that, Sergeant.'

'Any other news come in from down the line?' Egan asked. 'Are these the only cases we're going to have to deal with?'

'We've not received any reports from the patrols about anyone else trying to enter Wyoming. It would appear that Deadwood's quick action in closing up their town contained the spread of the disease.'

'I'd best get a move on, Cap. I've got a lot to do. As for the special chore you have in mind, I'll see about that tonight.'

'Good enough. I'll instruct Lieutenant Gordon to keep his sentries a safe distance from the Indian encampment,' Buckley said. 'I wouldn't want any of the men to be in a position where Yellow Hand and his braves could jump them.'

'Good thinking, Cap.'

'See you tomorrow then.'

Even as the sergeant rode away, Buckley was thinking of Yellow Hand. The vicious killer and his murderous band didn't deserve a life of leisure on some reservation. If he had been put in charge of their disposition, the only thing awaiting the chief and his assassins would have been a noose! Justice would have been served and the tortured souls of their numerous victims would have been able to rest in peace.

Buckley discovered he had his teeth clenched together so tightly it caused them to ache. Yellow Hand had destroyed his life. The murder of his wife and child had eaten away his conscience and put a black hole in his heart. No amount of retribution would ever compensate for his loss. He would never marry again and there would be no child to carry on the Buckley name. The cut-throat chief had destroyed him and his future. How befitting it would be if Buckley could find a way to return the favor.

The days dragged by at a snail's pace for Vance Jardeen. He did what he could, but it was a losing battle. His two patients suffered the usual torment from smallpox – a burning fever, which produced a rash, then progressed with the development of pus-filled blisters. The victims suffered from cramps and vomited until they were dehydrated and had no strength left in their body.

The only thing he could do for the pair was keep them warm and try to force liquids into them. The chore was equal to trying to stop the wind with a fishnet. On his fourth day, the elderly woman gave up the ghost and joined her husband in death. He buried her by his side and it left only the niece to care for.

Stormy remained in and out of delirium, tortured by body aches and in complete misery. As the blisters began to dry, he secured the woman's hands at her waist, to prevent her from scratching at her face. He knew such a reaction could leave scars from the pox. Her condition was critical, but she was a fighter. The lady had not regained full consciousness since the one time he had talked to her, so she had no way of knowing she was a lone survivor. That information might have caused her to lose her pluck and surrender to death's beckoning.

Vance looked after her often and spent the night at her side. He didn't wish for her to wake up and be alone. Every few hours, he would put water or broth to her lips and coax her to swallow a few drops. Eventually, the fever broke and she began to show signs of recovery.

When she became lucid, Vance was able to untie her wrists and feed her a small portion of solid food. After a full week had passed Stormy showed signs of improvement and started to regain her strength. The blisters dried up and began to flake off and she was able to speak in a hoarse whisper.

'I haven't asked,' she said to him, one dark evening, 'because I'm afraid I know the answer. My uncle and aunt?'

'I'm sorry,' Vance told her quietly. 'They didn't make it.'

The girl took the news without breaking down. She had obviously concluded they had not survived. Vance could offer no solace except to hold her hand.

Stormy mustered a weary, faint smile for him.

'I wouldn't have lived either, not without you being here.'

'Don't give me too much credit, ma'am. You fought long and hard to beat the smallpox.'

'Did you tell me your name?' she asked.

'Vance Jardeen,' he replied.

The girl gave a slight nod of her head. 'I remember now. It seems like weeks have passed since I came down with the fever.'

'Smallpox is about the worst disease there is,' Vance agreed.

'I'd like to pay my respects,' Stormy said. 'Would you help me?'

Vance assisted the young woman out of the wagon, then put an arm around her. She was quite unsteady and leaned on him for support.

They made their way to the pair of graves and Stormy said a prayer for her aunt and uncle. She had suffered physical pain, but the tragic loss of her relatives was equally devastating.

'I don't know what to do,' she confessed to Vance, after saying her goodbye. 'I've never been on my own before.'

'We'll sort it out at the next town,' he suggested. 'Or we might catch up with your wagon train.'

'We didn't really know any of those people,' she replied. 'We joined the train for protection, but we were not members of their religion, so we kept to ourselves. I think our isolation is part of why they left us behind. They thought we might not have had enough contact with them to spread the disease to any of the others.'

'If they were in Deadwood with you, they likely picked up the plague, same as your aunt and uncle. I'd guess they didn't get far before some of the others began showing sign of the disease.'

'It makes my situation rather difficult,' Stormy said. 'Where am I to go?'

'Something will turn up,' Vance told her. 'You've been very strong to this point. You need to keep up that strength for a bit longer.'

'I'll try,' she vowed.

Vance allowed the girl to rest for two more days. Then, when they were ready to travel, it was time to do a final sorry deed. After Vance had gathered up what little his horse could pack, besides the two of them, the wagon and all of the other belongings went up in a blazing fire. It was the only way to make sure someone didn't come along and go through the wagon and maybe catch the disease. Stormy ended up with only the clothes on her back, a change of unmentionables and a few toilet items.

As for the two of them, Vance also washed down his horse, then cleaned his blankets and everything else he owned. From the first time he had approached the wagon, he had been careful to only approach his horse to move him from one place to another and give him water. Being so careful, it was highly unlikely that the animal would have picked up any of the smallpox germs.

As they stood back to watch the raging fire, Vance shared the despair of the woman. She wrapped her arms about herself, as if she was cold. Watching the flames devour the wagon and all of her family's belongings caused tears to roll down her cheeks. She was desolate and alone.

'My only relatives or friends for more than four hundred miles are dead and gone,' she murmured. 'Where do I go from here?'

'You might still find your way over to Utah?'

'My uncle had friends and a cousin in Salt Lake. However, they were all on his side of the family, not mine. I don't know a soul, not even their names.'

'Well, Miss Malone, we've only got one horse. I was supposed to be at Fort Sage, over near Wayward, Wyoming, a week ago. I reckon you're stuck making the trip with me.'

'It seems the only choice I have. I can't very well walk to civilization.'

'Let's get moving then.'

The woman nodded, but he didn't miss the look of apprehension in her eyes. She'd lost her loved ones and everything she owned. Stormy had to be feeling very alone and vulnerable about now.

The authoritative-looking cavalry officer, probably in his mid-thirties, introduced himself as Captain Buckley. He offered no introduction for the two younger horse-soldiers with him, whose complete attention was directed to Miss Malone, rather than to what was being said.

Although dusty from riding and two days of travel, Stormy had weathered the pox with little outward evidence. Her face and arms were free of scabs and she was not altogether unattractive. With eligible girls in this part of the country about as rare as chicken-lips, she was going to garner a lot of attention.

'My condolences on the loss of your family, Miss Malone.' The captain spoke to her once Vance had explained her situation. 'The wagon train you spoke of didn't escape the smallpox. We have them quarantined a few miles back in the hills. They also have suffered considerable losses to this point. We expect fifty per cent or more to perish before this is finally over.'

'But you have been able to contain the outbreak?' Vance asked Captain Buckley.

'So it would seem, Mr Jardeen. We've received no reports of any other cases – either here in Wyoming or anywhere outside of Deadwood.'

'I explained to you about the precautions I took with Miss Malone,' Vance said. 'We should be free of any contamination.'

'I agree. And according to our surgeon, the victims who recover don't transmit the disease once they have been given clean clothes and taken proper baths.'

'We both washed until our skin was raw and my hair came out by the roots,' Stormy told the captain. 'I believe the soap Mr Jardeen carries is strong enough to remove a layer of rust.'

The captain nodded his satisfaction, then turned to Vance.

'I imagine you are eager to start processing the Indians?'

'That's my job. Once I have a full accounting, we can send for the troops who have been assigned to come and move them to the reservation.'

'Very good,' said Buckley crisply. 'If you should need anything from us, you only have to ask.'

'Thank you, Captain.'

'Were you intending to take the lady to Wayward before you start work?'

'Yes, I'd like to get her situated before I start with the processing.'

The officer glanced skyward. 'It's early yet, so you should be there well before dark. The main road forks ahead and the town is about twenty miles due south.' He glanced at Stormy again. 'I hope you'll be spared any more hardship, madam.'

Vance and Stormy both thanked the captain, then Vance headed his horse in the direction the man had indicated. He needed to find a place for the lady to stay. Hopefully, there would be an opportunity for a job or some place she could earn her room and board. If not... He didn't want to think along those lines. He had a job to do and he was already a full ten days behind schedule.

The ride took a little over four hours. As they entered town, Vance looked over the signs: the RED STEER SALOON, COW-POKE'S BEEF & BROTH, and the

54

RANCHER'S SAVINGS & LOAN. This was obviously cattle country.

The hotel was located in the middle of town. Vance rode over to the hitching-post and swung down. He barely had time to help Stormy to the ground before several men walked up to him. Two were smiling but not in a friendly way.

'Howdy, mister,' one of them said. 'You ain't one of them from those quarantine wagons, are you?'

Vance felt a sinking in his stomach. Why did it appear these guys had been waiting for him? He mustered a smile.

'Not us. The wagon train is the other side of the Fort.'

'Then you must be the Indian-lover,' the biggest of the men sneered. 'They call me Big Irish – Irish McCalegan. These are me mates: Topper, Jinx and Button.'

'I'm Vance Jardeen from–'

'We be knowing where you come from, Indian-lover.' Irish cut his reply short. 'It's where you're headed now that we be interested in.'

'I've got to process the Indians so we can escort them to the reservation.'

'Aye, the government is offering the Indians their own special paradise, where those heathen, murdering savages can hunt and fish till they are old and gray. Seems a slight bit of punishment for all their crimes and the number of people they have killed.'

Vance frowned. 'I don't know what you've heard about reservations, but I certainly wouldn't consider such a place a paradise.'

'Them murdering devils kilt me brother,' Irish said.

'My sister lost her whole family,' Topper joined in.

'I lost my uncle and two cousins,' Jinx added.

'And they murdered my folks,' Button finished the list of crimes. 'Along with that, some of those warriors are also part of the bunch who slaughtered General Custer and two hundred men from the Seventh Cavalry.'

'The fighting is over,' Vance replied carefully. 'Except for the Indians who escaped up into Canada, most of the others are already on reservations.'

'It's our thinking that them red-hides should be put to answer for their deeds,' Irish stated resolutely. 'Their women and children folk be free to go, but Yellow Hand and his warriors need to atone for the killing they done.'

'It was war,' Vance argued. 'They were fighting for what they considered to be their own land.'

'Sure,' Topper scoffed, 'as if a handful of nomad Indians have the right to claim a piece of the country bigger than most states. The government gives a farmer a hundred and sixty acres per family. Those savages want a hundred and sixty *square miles* ... each!'

'I am sorry for your losses,' Vance began, 'but my job is only to–'

Vance's words were cut off as Irish's fist shot out and struck him in the stomach. The blow doubled him over and knocked the wind from his lungs.

'You won't be saving the likes of Yellow Hand and his butchers so easily.' Irish snarled the words. 'It's a fine lesson you'll be learnin' today!'

Vance was trapped. He might have given Big Irish a battle, but the other three men attacked him, too. Stormy cried out for someone to help, but the sound of her voice was lost with a blow to his head.

Dark shadows and blinding flashes of light swirled violently in front of Vance's eyes. He couldn't focus on a target or strike back, being pummeled by four men at once. He

57

covered up as best he could, but the pounding came from all sides. When he felt his knees buckle, he wondered if he would ever regain consciousness.

Stormy charged at Big Irish, swinging at him with tightly balled fists. However, she was like a pesky horsefly to the man. He batted her hands away and eventually caught her by the wrists.

'Don't be for gettin' yourself mixed up in this, missy,' he snarled, shoving her away. 'We don't aim to kill your beau – not if we can help it.'

'He's done nothing to you!' Stormy cried. 'Leave him alone!'

'In due time, me pretty lass,' the big man said. Then he nodded to Topper. 'First off, we'll be showin' Mr Jardeen what we think of Indian-lovers.'

Stormy knew she could do nothing against four men. She hurried down the street to a building with a JAIL sign above the door. As the door was open, she ran inside.

'Afternoon, ma'am,' a lanky man said cordially. He was lounging behind a desk with a cup of coffee in one hand.

'There's a man being beaten up in the street!' she cried. 'You've got to help him!'

The lawman took a sip of his coffee.

'I wondered why Irish and the boys were hanging around town. I reckon you're concerned about that there Indian representative or whatever he is.'

'You've got to do something! They're going to kill him!'

'Irish ain't the sort to kill anyone, ma'am. I reckon they're just letting off a little steam over the fact them Indians are going to get away with their crimes.'

'What kind of lawman are you?' she demanded to know. 'There are four of them, beating up on one lone man!'

'I'm the kind who has buried a good many Indian victims – men, women and children. Some bodies didn't even look human, after being tortured and mutilated by those savages. As for Irish and his pals, they are the ranchers who pay the taxes that pays my salary. I can't very well go up against the men who hired me.'

'What a sniveling coward you are!'

'Light down from offa my back, woman,' the man growled. 'This here is cattle country and we've done battled those red devils for the last ten years. If you don't like the way things stack up here, you sure don't have to set down no roots!'

Stormy didn't argue with the man further.

She whirled about and returned to the street in time to see Vance going past – dragged behind a horse!

Stormy searched about, desperate to find help. Then she spied two young men coming out of the nearby saloon.

'Please!' she cried, hurrying over to them. 'Can you help me?'

The pair paused long enough to look after Vance being dragged up the street.

'Let me guess,' one said drily, 'that's your man the one on the wrong end of the rope?'

She put an imploring look on them.

'I owe that man for saving my life. Won't you please help?'

'Topper won't drag him far,' the second man told her. 'I'm sure they don't intend to kill him.'

'Please!' Stormy beseeched them a second time.

'I reckon Irish and his boys won't mind if we help you pick up whatever pieces are left of your fella,' the first one answered. 'That suit you, ma'am?'

'Oh, yes! Thank you!'

The same one gave a nod to the second fellow.

'You follow after them, Rick,' he told him. 'I'll hitch up one of our wagons and we'll be along as quick as we can.'

'OK, Tom,' the other replied. 'I'll trail along till Topper cuts him loose.'

Rick grabbed up a horse from the nearby hitching-post, swung aboard and rode out of town at a gallop. Tom, meanwhile, led the way toward the livery. He spoke to Stormy as they hurried their step.

'Don't worry, ma'am,' he told her. 'Irish and his pals ain't cold-blooded killers. They're just expressing their frustration.'

'And you're not a cattleman?' she asked.

'Nope. Me and my brother are teamsters. We live about a half-mile out of town. We've been holed up on this side of the border, until the smallpox thing is cleared up at Deadwood. They aren't allowing anyone to cross into the Dakotas until that there disease has run its course.'

'And you have a wagon?'

'I'll hitch up a team right quick and we'll get after Rick and your husband,' Tom assured her. 'Like I said, Topper won't drag him for more than a short way.'

'Please hurry,' Stormy urged, not bothering to tell him that Vance Jardeen wasn't her husband. There would be time for sorting out details afterward.

CHAPTER FOUR

When Stormy and Tom arrived on the buck-board, Rick was by the side of the road, standing over Vance's unconscious body. Stormy jumped down and rushed over to kneel at his side. The two brothers stood silently by as she began gently to examine him.

'I don't understand why they did this to him,' she lamented. 'He didn't do anything to those men!'

'I didn't find any broken bones,' Rick said. 'Least ways, none was sticking out through the skin.'

'Where can we take him?' Stormy asked. 'I'm going to need some water and band-ages.'

'We can haul him over to our house,' Tom offered. 'Ma's got the fixings to patch him up.'

Stormy looked over at him. 'I hate to impose on you further, but I would truly appreciate it.'

'Think nothing of it, ma'am,' Tom said,

displaying a tight grin. 'We'd have likely done the same thing without your asking.'

Stormy followed along as Tom and Rick carried Vance over to the back of the wagon. Then she climbed in first and sat down, so she could cradle his head on her lap.

'Where are you staying, ma'am?' Rick asked.

'We had only just arrived in town. We were going to try and find a room at a hotel or boarding-house.'

'Maybe Ma can help with that too,' Tom said. 'With us boys gone most of the time, she could use a house guest. We've an empty room too.'

'I'm afraid for Mr Jardeen,' Stormy told him. 'He's covered with scrapes and bruises. After being beaten and dragged behind a horse, he's lucky to even be alive!'

Tom climbed aboard and took up the reins to the horse. He started the team moving and cocked his head to speak over his shoulder.

'There's still a lot of hard feelings toward the Indians out at Camp Sage,' he said. 'A good many folks think the warriors who were involved in local attacks or killings ought to be hanged or imprisoned.'

'Mr Jardeen is here to send them to a

63

reservation,' Stormy replied to that. 'The braves are free to roam, but they're not allowed to leave the reservation. Their days of fighting and killing are over.'

'Big Irish and the others don't see it that way,' Tom said.

Rick rode alongside the wagon. After a short way, he also spoke to Stormy.

'Was I you,' he said, 'I wouldn't be real vocal about defending the Indians around town. Some folks are a little touchy in that area.'

She pulled a face. 'There's a piece of information Mr Jardeen could have used fifteen minutes ago.'

'Yes, ma'am.'

'We'll be to the house in about fifteen minutes,' Tom informed her. 'Like I said earlier, our place is about a half-mile the other side of town.'

'Please hurry.'

Rick gave a nod of his head. 'He's going to be OK, ma'am,' he said. 'He looks like he's got some bark on his hide.'

'Maybe so, but most of his hide was scraped off while he was being dragged.'

'Yes, ma'am.'

Then the two brothers ceased talking.

Stormy felt completely helpless, unable to

do anything for Vance but cushion his head on the ride. She uttered up a silent prayer asking God to look after this man who had saved her own life.

At the Markley home, Stormy discovered the two boys' mother to be a fairly stout woman, rather unsmiling and gruff on the surface. However, she seemed genuinely concerned about the comfort and welfare of her guests. She helped Stormy clean and bandage the worst of Vance's injuries. By the time they were finished, he was wrapped up with a dozen different bandages.

'I seen worse that managed to survive,' the woman said, after the job was complete. 'He'll be OK.'

'Goodness!' Stormy exclaimed. 'How does someone end up in worse condition than a man who is beaten and dragged?'

'There was one time, when a fellow's horse went down in the middle of a cattle stampede. He must have been stepped on fifty times, but he come through it with only the loss of several teeth and the loss of hearing in one ear.'

'Sounds dreadful.'

'Working cattle ain't for sissies,' the woman said with a grunt.

Vance heard the distant voices and fought

to become conscious. He managed to open his eyes and shut them against a sudden, knifelike pain that ripped through his skull.

'Vance?' Stormy spoke softly to him. 'Are you awake? Can you hear me?'

It caused a wave of agony, but he managed to bob his head up and down.

'My head feels like a split melon,' he murmured.

'You have a nasty bruise on your forehead,' Stormy told him.

Vance paused to take a deep breath. There was an ache along his ribs, but no sharp, penetrating pain. He was no doctor, but he guessed his injuries to be a concussion and possibly a couple of cracked ribs. Everything else seemed to work.

'Guess I'll live,' he muttered, reopening his eyes and trying to focus his vision.

Besides Stormy, nearby were two young men and an older woman. One of the boys grinned, seeing him come awake.

'Seen me a photograph of a mummy one time,' he said. 'He didn't have so many bandages as you.'

'I do figure I know what a birthday present feels like,' Vance replied.

'Was my man still around, he'd have put a stop to Irish and the others,' the elderly woman spoke firmly. 'No one messed with my Calvin, not even Big Irish.'

'That's our mom,' the boy said. Then he took time to introduce himself, his brother and their mother.

'Pa died last fall,' Rick explained to Vance. 'Got stepped on by a horse and it busted him up inside. Weren't nothing the doctor could do.'

'Now it's only me and my boys,' Mrs Markley said. 'At least, until one of them finds a gal and settles down. Being teamsters, I don't know when or if that will ever happen.'

'Ma worries about us some,' Rick agreed.

'How about you and your missus?' Mrs Markley asked. 'You two been married long?'

Vance arched his brows at her question.

'Uh, we're not married.'

That brought a frown to her face.

'But we thought that—'

'I'm sorry,' Stormy said at once. 'With all of the excitement, I didn't correct your son when he referred to Mr Jardeen as my husband.'

'Miss Malone was traveling with her uncle,' Vance said quickly. 'The man died in a wagon mishap and I was trying to help her get settled. She had to leave most of her belongings behind.'

'Then you're a woman left on your own,' Mrs Markley said almost gently.

'Yes,' Stormy said, casting a sharp look at Vance, 'that's pretty much the truth.'

'It's fortunate Mr Jardeen happened along to see to your welfare. This is a hard and dangerous land to travel alone.'

'What about these cattlemen?' Vance changed the subject. 'Is there a chance they might attack the Indians at Camp Sage?'

'You got a taste of their feelings today,' Tom said. 'However, the army has positioned itself between the hate of the local people and the chance of any revenge. Big Irish and his friends aren't going to tackle an armed force to get at the Indians.'

'Yeah, that's probably the reason they struck out at you – because they can't get at the Indians themselves,' Rick deduced.

'Well, I'm only here to process those people, not involve myself in a war which ended with Yellow Hand's surrender,' Vance said.

That brought a coarse laugh from Mrs Markley. 'There's more than a few folks around who feel there isn't any justice for the murder of their friends and family members.

Whether you think so or not, you're caught smack in the middle, Mr Indian agent.'

'I work for the Bureau of Indian Affairs,' he corrected. 'I'm not an Indian agent.'

The woman snorted her scepticism.

'You can pass that along to Big Irish, but I doubt it will make much difference.'

'It's late and about time we turned in,' Rick spoke up.

'I prepared a room for a husband and wife,' Mrs Markley said. 'I didn't know you two weren't married.'

'The way I'm feeling, I think I'll be able to sleep anywhere I can lie down,' Vance said. 'I hate to put you folks out.'

'We'll bunk him with us.' Rick grinned. 'He can sleep between me and Tom. He might be good for warming feet in the middle of the night.'

Mrs Markley chuckled. 'Better that you boys make him a bunk on the back porch. Wouldn't want you disturbing his sleep with your big hoofs.'

'Yeah, Ma,' Rick agreed. 'Besides which, he might be ticklish and keep us all awake.'

Vance had no choice but to spend the night, but he decided to move into town the next day. The two boys were at home and, with Mrs Markley offering Stormy room and board, they didn't have enough space for him. He would sleep out on the back porch, then manage to find something else come morning.

He made the stiff and awkward trip to the door, leading out to the porch, when Stormy came over to speak to him.

'You didn't have to make up a white lie about me,' she whispered. 'I could have told them the truth, that my aunt and uncle died from smallpox.'

Vance kept his voice hushed. 'People are terrified of that pestilence, Stormy. If you mentioned your bout with smallpox, we might have both ended up sleeping under the stars. Fear of a deadly disease causes even good people to become harsh and in-humane. Remember how those people from the wagon train took your horses and left you stranded to die. They weren't a bunch of vicious killers. They were religious people, but they were terrified of having anyone around with such a deadly disease. And, although you are well now, a lot of people would still be fearful they might be able to catch smallpox from you.'

'I don't like lying about it,' she said.

'It isn't that far from the truth,' he argued. 'Besides, it's only until you get settled and figure a way to take care of yourself. Then, if you feel the need, you can tell Mrs Markley the truth.'

Stormy sighed wearily. Vance gave her an appraising glance.

Standing in the glow of the room's lamp, her features illuminated by the soft light, he was struck by her sweet candor. She was still on the frail side, weakened from her deathly bout with smallpox. But she had escaped with few visible marks of the disease and was as lovely as a painting.

'I lived with my parents, then with my uncle and his wife,' she murmured, breaking into his thoughts. 'I've never had to be on my own or make my own decisions.'

'You must feel a terrible sense of being alone,' Vance said. 'I know the feeling. I lost most of my family about a dozen years back.'

'Didn't you tell me it was smallpox too?'

'Yes. My father survived for a couple years, but I had to take care of him.'

'You have come a long way for a man on his own.'

'And I'm sure you'll find a new life for yourself too. It might take a little time, but you'll find it soon enough.'

'What about your job?' she asked. 'Are you

going to end up taking more beatings and possibly get yourself killed?'

'Soon as I can get around without staggering, I'll finish my job. Once the Indians are accounted for, they will be escorted to their reservation. You heard Mrs Markley. Big Irish and the others aren't going to challenge the army for a little revenge.'

Stormy looked him over. He was covered with scratches and bruises, but he was able to stand. He'd been lucky this time.

'It appears your bed is ready,' she said, seeing Rick and Tom head out to the bunkhouse.

'Yes, I feel like I could sleep for a week.'

'Will I see you in the morning?' Stormy asked.

'I don't know. I've got to get into town first thing and send off a wire to my boss. He is going to be wondering what happened to me.'

'I'll just say good-night then,' she said.

He told her 'good-night', then turned and stiffly made his way out to the back porch. He wondered if he was missing something. Stormy was a special lady, sweet, charming and beautiful inside. He was warmed at the notion of how she had held his head on her lap and tended to his injuries. What if there was a chance for something more between them?

Vance shook the thought from his mind. Whatever kindness she had shown him had likely been due to gratitude.

He couldn't take advantage of her for that. She plainly felt indebted to him for his tending to her. Well, she had repaid that debt by doing the same for him. They were even. Strangely, he didn't care for the conclusion, not one little bit.

Vance found a room at the hotel the next day. Though unsteady at times, he managed to get around on his own. After seeing to his horse, he went to the freight office and sent off a wire to his home office, advising them of the delay in processing the Indians. Next, he bought himself a new suit of clothes and then returned to his room and rested up for a couple of hours. He left the hotel that afternoon in time to meet Captain Buckley, who had ridden up to the hotel hitching-post. He waited while the man dismounted from his horse and stepped across to look him over.

'I heard about your trouble, Jardeen. Tough luck, running into those ranchers. I should have warned you about them, but I didn't believe they'd get rough with you, especially with you escorting a lady.'

'They pretty much left her out of it. I can respect them for that. As for the rest...?' Vance shrugged. 'Maybe I'll get the chance to settle the score between us before I leave.'

Buckley changed the subject. 'Did you telegraph in your resignation?'

'No, I've still got a job to do. I let the department know that I was running a few days behind schedule. I didn't want them thinking I'd gotten lost or something.'

'How long will it take to process the tribe?'

'Depends on how many Indians there are to register. We need a full accounting before we can move them.'

'To prevent any possible attacks by the local people, I'm proposing we encircle the Indian camp with a fence. It will not only ensure the Indians don't sneak away during the night, but it will also prevent any men like Big Irish and his friends from being able to attack them.'

'That sounds like a lot of work,' Vance replied to the idea. 'Especially when I should be finished in a week or ten days.'

'You don't appear ready to ride just yet.'

'I should be able to make the trip in a couple days – soon as I can sit a horse for more than a few minutes without doubling over or falling off from being dizzy,' Vance answered.

'It does appear you got a pretty good knock to the head.'

Vance touched the knot on the right side of his forehead.

'Yeah, I don't feel ready to butt heads with a mountain goat just yet.'

'Probably received a concussion,' Buckley said. 'I could have the post surgeon ride into town and look you over.'

'No need, Captain. I'll rest up until I can safely sit a horse.'

Buckley accepted his explanation with a bob of his head.

'Well, to ensure you have no more problems while you're here, I've brought in Corporal Dowd and a couple of our men. They will see you are not molested a second time.'

'I don't know that it's necessary, but I do appreciate the consideration.'

The captain waved to three nearby troopers and turned for his horse.

'I'll see you when you arrive at Camp Sage, Mr Jardeen. Good luck.'

Vance said goodbye to him and was joined by a friendly-looking corporal and two privates.

'You look a lot better than I might have guessed,' the corporal said, showing a grin. 'After hearing about your little ride, I expected to find you in two or three large pieces.'

'I might be, if it wasn't for all the bandages holding me together under my clothes,' Vance replied. 'I've more cuts and scratches than an old sofa in a house full of cats.'

The young man laughed. 'I can believe that. I'm Corporal Dowd.' He introduced himself. 'These two troopers are Hines and Graft.'

'Vance Jardeen,' Vance replied back. 'I'm sorry you boys are stuck on such a worth-nothing detail,' he went on. 'I don't think anyone is going to give me any more trouble.'

'We don't mind being in town for a couple days.' Dowd winked. 'And there's always the nights to look forward to.'

'Well, I'm still sorry to put you boys out,' Vance said.

'Beats the detail I was on,' the corporal said. 'I've been over helping tend to a wagon train of smallpox victims. That's one sorry detail.'

'You've had the disease then?'

The man pointed to his face. 'I didn't get these pockmarks from washing with cactus.

I lost a little brother and my mother to that rotten pestilence.'

'I fared little better myself,' Vance replied. 'How are the people doing at the wagon train?'

'Nearly everyone on the train came down sick. I'd say they will have lost about half of their number before this is over. I'll be a happy man if I never have to smell the stench of smallpox or burnt human flesh again.'

'Cremation is safer than burying the bodies, I guess.'

'Yes, we can't risk an animal digging them up. We would have had to plant the bodies deep and there were simply too many victims for that kind of burial. Fire is the safest and quickest way to go.'

Vance suffered a wave of despair. 'I'm surprised the army could spare you. I don't imagine your post has all that many men who have survived smallpox.'

'It's mostly clean-up at this point,' Dowd said. 'A good many of the pilgrims are recovered now and tending to their own. I think the captain offered me this detail as a reward for the misery I've seen the past couple weeks.'

'Then the disease has pretty much run its course?'

'Yep. Soon as the three-week quarantine is up, there will only be the clean-up work to do.'

'They've suffered a tough break,' Vance said.

'Once they renew their supplies and re-organize, they are continuing their journey. The survivors are a tough bunch. They still intend to get to Utah and settle there. I swear, those souls are hardy enough to wade through about anything.'

'What a tragic waste of human lives,' Vance said with a shake of his head. 'If there's anything worse than smallpox, I hope I never have to see it.'

'That's sure enough the truth,' the corporal agreed. Then his gaze shifted up the street to where a wagon had stopped.

Vance turned to see Stormy and Mrs Markley climb down from the wagon. They walked together toward the first business along the main street. Mrs Markley was obviously going to introduce Stormy around and try to help her find a job.

'Say!' Dowd exclaimed, whistling under his breath, 'who's the new gal in town?'

'Stormy Malone,' Vance replied. 'She lost her wagon and uncle a few days back. She came in with me.'

Dowd looked at him. 'She your gal?'

The question caught Vance unprepared.

'Uh, not exactly,' he muttered. 'We're just friends.'

The corporal chuckled. 'See what I was saying? Things are looking up about this detail already!'

Vance frowned at the corporal's enthusiasm, as they all watched Stormy disappear into a shop. With little money or possessions, Stormy needed to find some way to provide for herself. It was going to be hard on her, but there was little time to mourn her loss or cuss the bad luck. Life went on, and time waited for no one.

However, his concern was not only for her welfare. At the moment, he felt an unsettling he could not fathom. He had eaten a full breakfast, yet he seemed to be suffering from hunger pangs. What the devil did that mean?

CHAPTER FIVE

The lieutenant frowned upon hearing the order.

'We are already short of men, Captain,' he said. 'Are you sure a fence is necessary?'

'I aim to control these savages, Lieutenant.'

'And Colonel Voight?' he asked. 'Does he know we are going to construct a fence around the Indian encampment?'

Buckley avoided a direct answer to the question.

'I shall see to it that not one single warrior sneaks away from the compound to make trouble. The man from Indian Affairs is expected to start processing Yellow Hand and his people within the week. It is my responsibility that there be a complete accounting of every one of those blood-thirsty savages. The number will be correct and complete!'

'Yes, I understand, Captain, but isn't this a waste of time? After all, we've got the Indians under constant surveillance and we're only talking a few more days. Why go to all the trouble of surrounding them with a barbed-wire fence?'

'I told you, Lieutenant, I'm taking no chances.'

'Whatever you say, sir.'

'The load of wire will be delivered this afternoon. See that the detail has heavy work-gloves and tools for the job.'

'Very good, Captain. I'll see the job gets done.'

Buckley watched him walk away. With the Indian Bureau man delayed a couple more days, it ought to be enough. The thought caused adrenalin to pump through his veins. He felt the rush of excitement. If his strategem worked, his overall plan would soon be in full operation. Once initiated, it would be too late to alter fate. No government-appointed Indian-lover was going to undo what he had in mind.

Stormy paused to mop her brow. Her hair was pinned back from her face, but lay pasted to her head from perspiration. There was a dampness under her arms and about her back and chest from the sweltering task. She paused from her labor to move over to the window. There was but a slight stir of

81

air, not enough of a breeze to help cool the oven-like back room of the laundry.

The small stove didn't give off a lot of heat, but Stormy had to stand next to it hour after hour, in order to constantly warm the two hand-irons. There seemed to be a mountain of laundry to be pressed. The bulk of the work was military uniforms, mostly from officers and a few men who cared enough to shell out the money for outside cleaning. It afforded the local laundry a good business, but pressing the military creases took time and a hot iron.

With a sigh of resignation, Stormy returned to the ironing-board. She sprinkled a bit of water and starch over a pair of trousers and then began to stroke the material with the iron, careful to put a crease in the right spot. As she worked, her mind turned over her limited options.

While this was a job, it didn't pay but a few cents more than what she would owe Mrs Markley for room and board each week. There was nothing bright about her future in Wayward, unless she was to wed one of the local bachelors.

With a steady diligence, Stormy continued laboring with the heavy iron. Meanwhile, she thought of what could have been a new life, a fresh start. Her aunt and uncle would have put her up until she decided what she would do with her life. It had seemed the answer to her prayers. She had longed for some adventure in her life, for a break from the daily boredom of living. Now she wished she could turn back the clock and return home to Kansas. There she had been the object of suitors – mostly farmers – a couple rather genial and handsome, while another two or three were the type who would have been dependable and utterly faithful husbands. She had resisted any opportunity of love, for she had vowed not to wed a farmer. The life was too hard, too solitary and dependent upon the elements. She didn't wish to watch her children die from lack of food or freeze in the cold of winter. She wanted something more.

But all of her dreams had changed now. Stormy found herself wondering about what sort of men lived around Wayward. She had seen for herself that some of them were brutes, like the men who beat up and then dragged Vance behind a horse. There was also the town marshal, a man who turned his back on a beating. What if all of the men this far West were like them? What if all of the men here lacked the decency and honor of a man like Vance?

The thought of him caused her to pause. He had moved to town after that first night and she had not seen him since she took the job at the laundry. He would soon be recovered from his injuries and start his work out at the army post. She wondered if he was even aware of the fact that she had taken on a job.

Stormy paused to change irons, placing the cool one on the stove to reheat. She adjusted the folded cloth, which she wrapped around the handle to protect her hand from the heat, then picked up the hot iron and began to press the item of clothing once more.

She worked more diligently than before, her brow creased in thought. Returning to her introspection about Vance, she definitely felt a stir of emotions around him. He had yet to say anything to show that he had more than a passing interest in her, but she had, on occasion, observed an ardent glimmer in his eyes. He often looked at her with a subtle tenderness and, when he spoke to her, he seemed to soften his words a bit more than he did for other people. However, a gentle word or gesture was not an invitation to romance. A person could not make a salad out of oak-leaves. She needed something more concrete.

Shaking the notion aside, Stormy harshly reminded herself that Vance would not be staying in Wayward. Once his job of processing the Indians for relocation was complete, he would leave and never return. It did no good to pine over a man who would soon be out of her life.

Bonnie, the owner of the laundry, entered the room to interrupt her contemplation. She looked over the pile of clothes that Stormy had finished and uttered a grunt of acknowledgment.

'Not bad for your first day,' she said. 'Do you think you want to do this six days a week?'

'I had to leave behind most everything I owned, after losing the wagon,' Stormy admitted. 'I'm rather desperate for a job.'

'I don't know, Stormy,' the woman said, peering at her with a narrow gaze. 'You look a mite peaked to me. This is hard and physical work. Are you sure you can handle this?'

'I'm still a bit worn out from the long days of travel,' Stormy excused her appearance. 'I'm sure I can do you a fair day's work.'

'OK, you got yourself a job. First of the

month is when the soldier boys get paid. I'll give you half-pay each week and then catch your wages up when I collect from them. I expect you to put in ten hours each day, other than for Sundays. We start at seven and you can leave at five-thirty. You can stop a half-hour about the middle of the shift to rest and have something to eat.'

'I understand.'

The woman started to walk out, then stopped in the doorway.

'You got enough clothes to wear till Saturday?'

'I ... I'm staying with Mrs Markley. I can wash what I'm wearing at nights until...'

'If you're not too proud for second-hand clothing, I've got a few items that have been left here and never been picked back up. We can look through the discards tomorrow and see if we can find you a couple work dresses that'll fit you.'

'That would be very helpful right now,' Stormy said quietly, a bit embarrassed by her ragged appearance.

Bonnie grunted. 'Well, I can see one other thing you bring to my business.'

'What's that?'

'I've had no less than ten new customers stop by today to leave a shirt or suit of clothes.' When Stormy frowned in puzzlement, Bonnie explained. 'There ain't exactly a bounty of eligible gals around. All of them new customers were men, betwixt the ages of twenty and Moses.' She flashed a smirk that was probably as close to a smile as ever crossed her aged face. 'Helps pay for your keep, all of them would-be suitors coming round.'

'I had no idea,' Stormy said, uncomfortable at suddenly finding herself so popular.

'You mark my words, gal, you'll be hitched before next spring.'

Stormy didn't reply to that, while the woman pulled a timepiece from her apron pocket. She squinted at it for a second,

'It's close enough to quitting time,' she stated, 'Put away the irons for the day. I'll have the stove stoked and burning hot by the time you get here tomorrow.'

Stormy hurried to do as she was told. It felt as if the weariness would buckle her legs, as she was still weak from her near-fatal bout with smallpox. But she had no choice. She was determined to pay her own way.

'There's a fella out front waiting for you,' Bonnie said. 'I told him you'd be a few minutes yet.'

'Thank you again, Bonnie.'

'You go ahead,' the older woman said gruffly. 'I'll finish up for you today.'

Stormy thanked her again, removed her work apron and hurried out of the laundry.

Vance saw her come through the door and moved stiffly forward. Stormy quickly put both hands up to her hair, trying to push it into place and make it neater. It was not much use, for she had been perspiring and the dampness made it hopelessly frizzy.

As her gaze met his own, she flashed him a bright smile. He wondered how she managed to find the strength.

'I must look like I've been drubbed through Bonnie's wash-tub and left out to dry in the wind,' Stormy said in greeting him. 'I kind of feel the same way too.'

'It must be like doing the devil's laundry, confined in a tiny room with a hot stove burning all day.'

She mustered a cheerful mien. 'I suspect it will be more comfortable in the winter months.'

He shook his head, wishing he knew of an easier job for her.

'How much is she paying you?'

'About two dollars a week. Mrs Markley allowed I could stay at her place, with room and board, for six dollars a month. I guess I won't have a lot of money to waste on incidentals.'

'And I thought army pay was wretched, but even a private gets sixteen dollars a month and keep,' he replied.

'I'll get by,' she said readily. 'At least I can earn a living.'

Vance could not hide the regret in his voice. 'Slaving over hot irons and suffering from the heat, it'll make you an old woman before your years.'

'Life goes on, Mr Jardeen. I must do whatever is necessary in order to survive.'

Instead of walking Stormy toward a horse or wagon, so he could escort her to the Markley place, Vance took her arm and led her toward the mercantile store.

'I thought you might need to stop by the store and pick up a few things,' he explained. 'We left behind most everything you owned, so you're bound to be short of a few items.'

'I don't wish to go into debt. I will hardly make enough at the laundry to pay for my room and board.'

'I spoke to the storekeeper,' he said. 'The man offered to allow you to carry up to twenty dollars on credit. Once you get on your feet, you can repay him a little at a time.'

'If I spent twenty dollars, it would take me months to repay him!' she exclaimed.

'He's not going anywhere,' Vance told her. 'Besides, a smart store-owner often grants a new arrival a little credit until they get settled.'

'I still don't feel right about this.'

Vance continued to escort her to the door of the mercantile.

'You have to at least get the necessities.'

Stormy sighed. 'Well, I hate having to borrow everything from Mrs Markley. I could use a brush, some hairpins, a couple of ribbons and some toiletry items.'

'You might want to pick out some comfortable shoes, stockings and whatever else you need, too,' Vance told her. 'I looked over the prices and it appears twenty dollars will be enough to get you set up proper.'

'Yes, but it's still more money than I'll make in two months.'

'Like I said, you can repay it a little at a time. You go ahead and pick up the things you're going to need.'

Stormy opened her mouth to protest again, but Vance opened the door and cocked his head.

'In you go.'

After a moment's hesitation, Stormy entered the store.

Vance remained on the walk. He surmised a woman would rather shop for personal things by herself, so he closed the door behind her and turned to wait.

However, he was met at once by an unfriendly face – it was Topper! With a quick, sweeping glance, Vance saw Jinx too, not thirty feet away. Big Irish was not in sight, but his two friends appeared primed for a fight.

Vance was wearing his gun, but he was no match for two of them. Even if he killed one, the other would surely cut him down. He took a deep breath and turned to meet them.

'Howdy, boys,' he said. 'You come to see I got home safely?'

'It appears you don't take a hint, Injun-lover,' Topper sneered. 'I figured that little ride we gave you out of town ought to have convinced you it wasn't healthy to hang your hat in this neck of the woods.'

'Maybe he needs a more permanent lesson,' suggested Jinx, his hand resting on the butt of his gun. 'You can turn tail and run, if you ain't got the stomach for dying.'

Topper nodded his agreement. 'As long as

you don't stop till you're out of Wyoming, we'll let you go.'

'I didn't come to Wyoming to fight with you men,' Vance said. 'I'm only here to process the Indians so they can be moved. You ought to be glad to have the Indian wars behind you.'

'What we don't like,' Topper sneered the words, 'is the fact those murdering savages are getting away with the killing of our friends and neighbors. What kind of justice is there in that?'

'They can make the same claim about the white men,' Vance said, hoping to avoid a showdown. 'Give me a couple days to do my job and you'll be rid of the Indians and me for ever.'

'Even one day is more than you're going to get!' Jinx snapped. 'You turn tail and git, or else we'll cut you down with a few pieces of lead!'

Vance saw the town marshal standing across the street. It was evident the man didn't intend to intervene. The fight was his own, whether he wanted it or not.

'Hate to butt in on you boys' private affairs.' An outside voice suddenly spoke up. 'But we need to talk to Mr Jardeen.'

All eyes turned to the speaker. Corporal

Dowd and two soldiers were poised, ready to take action in any kind of fight. The corporal looked right at Topper and Jinx. 'You don't mind if we have a chat with your friend here, do you?' Dowd asked them both.

'We ain't discussing no army business,' Topper warned him. 'You'd best keep your nose out of this!'

Dowd gave his head a negative shake.

'Sorry, Topper,' he said, 'but I've got my orders. This man is under army protection until he processes the Indian people at Camp Sage.'

'Army protection?' Topper said.

'That's right. You boys wouldn't want to interfere in army business now, would you?'

Topper and Jinx exchanged glances.

'We'll see what Big Irish has to say about this,' Topper snapped.

'Big Irish doesn't hold any rank in the army,' the corporal said evenly. 'But you boys can do whatever you want, so long as you don't interfere with Mr Jardeen's business.'

Confusion covered the faces of the two cowmen. They had expected to push Vance into a fight and perhaps injure or even kill him. Now the army was backing him. It was more of a job than they were prepared for. With a pair of threatening looks, the two men spun around and walked away.

Vance sighed his relief, while his heart slowed to beat normally and the strength returned to his knees.

'Who says the cavalry doesn't arrive on time?' he spoke to the corporal.

'Never heard anyone say that before,' Dowd told him with a grin.

'You risked your necks just now. I appreciate your help.'

'Captain Buckley sent us to see you didn't milk your injuries for a month. He wants to be rid of Yellow Hand and his people before winter sets in.'

'Yellow Hand does not seem to be popular with anyone around here.'

'There's a lot of hate in the valley for him and his warriors,' Dowd replied. 'Can't really blame them, I suppose. Most people here about lost friends and relatives during the past few years of fighting. You're in the middle of a war that's been raging in this valley for a long time.'

'I'd say the army is in the middle too.' Vance said.

'Yeah, we're stuck watching over Yellow Hand and his tribe until they are processed and moved to a reservation.'

'Thanks again for your help. I owe you.'

'Well, looking out for you is kind of secondary to my real purpose,' Dowd said with a wink. 'I've been trying to meet the new gal you brung to town. I don't suppose you'd like to introduce me?'

'She just put in a full day's work at the laundry, Dowd. I don't know how sociable she is feeling right now.'

'Think she'd be interested in an army rooster like myself?'

Vance forced a smile to his face, but another of those annoying knots returned to form in his stomach.

'I don't know, Corporal. I haven't asked what kind of man she might be interested in.'

'If you're not up to a ride, I'd be happy to round up a wagon and see the lady gets to the Markley place OK.'

'I've staked out the job for the night,' Vance replied. 'Maybe some other time.'

'Yeah, OK,' the young man said. 'You watch your back, Jardeen. Big Irish and his boys might still be looking for their pound of flesh.'

'I figure I already gave about that much on my belly-ride out of town. Still, I'll keep a sharp eye for them.'

The corporal nodded to his two men, and the three of them moved along down the street. Vance was beholden to the corporal for possibly saving his life, but, as for the issue of courting Stormy – that was something else again.

Colonel Voight regarded Captain Buckley with a curious suspicion.

'Lieutenant Gordon informed me of your plan,' he said. 'Are you quite certain enclosing the Indian encampment with barbed wire is necessary?'

'Yes, sir,' Buckley said firmly. 'I have received intelligence from one of our informants that Yellow Hand intends to take out a raiding party before we can relocate his people.'

'I've heard no such rumor.'

'Some Indians will talk only to certain people. Sergeant Egan has contacts inside the Indian camp. They have assured him that some kind of mischief is in the works.'

'I see,' the colonel said.

'If I might suggest, Colonel, I should be in complete charge of overseeing the Indians. The smallpox epidemic has been contained. Word arrived yesterday that Deadwood has lifted its quarantine. It would seem the disease is no longer a threat.'

The colonel gave a thoughtful bob of his head.

'What about this Jardeen fellow, from the War Department? Have you received word about when he will be ready to process and relocate Yellow Hand's people?'

'It will be another day or two before he can start. Then it will take him a week or ten days for his processing. I know the fence and our continued vigilance might seem a waste of time, but–'

The colonel lifted a hand to stop further explanation.

'Very well, Captain. You are in charge of the Indian camp. You do whatever you deem necessary. I expect you to see that the rations are issued promptly and that none of the warriors escapes custody. The responsibility for those people rests squarely on your shoulders.'

'I welcome the task and assume total responsibility, Colonel.'

'All right, Captain.' He dismissed the subject. 'You see to the Indians and have Lieutenant Gordon continue to monitor the patrols and check on any travelers entering this part of the country. With any luck, this outbreak will be contained and over with in a very short while.'

'Yes, sir.'

'That's all, Captain.'

Buckley came to attention and snapped a salute. When the colonel returned the gesture, he spun smartly to the door and left the office. By the time he reached his horse, ideas were swirling about in his head.

For a brief moment, he had been afraid the colonel would relieve him of the duty of watching over Yellow Hand. Such an action would have ruined his plan for the future ... a plan he intended to see through to the end. At last, after all the long, endless months of suffering and biding his time, the butchers of his wife and son were going to pay their due!

Vance was too stiff to ride for more than a few minutes yet, but he made the trip from town without a lot of discomfort. With Stormy riding in front of him, he turned up the lane toward the Markley house. He wondered at the girl's sullen silence.

'Is something the matter?' he asked. 'You haven't said a word since we left town.'

'I'm quite tired. I don't think I was ready to tackle the type of physical work that Bonnie expects a person to handle in one day.'

'I wish there was a better job for you. But with the wives of the soldiers available for steady work, there aren't many jobs available. Not to mention, Wayward isn't on any major shipping lines. This valley is rather isolated from the rest of Wyoming.'

'I'll get by,' Stormy said.

He wasn't satisfied by her answer, but she'd have been a good card-player. She hid her feelings very well. Only the droop of her shoulders gave away how tired she was from working ten hours.

'I wish I could help,' Vance said.

Stormy glanced back over her shoulder at him, a spark igniting in the depths of her eyes.

'You've done more than you should.'

He began, 'I've only done–'

But she broke in to stop his reply. 'And please don't spend any more of your money on me.'

'What do you mean?' he asked, trying to sound innocent.

'You know very well what I mean!' She bit off the statement sharply. 'The storekeeper didn't tell his wife about the arrangement you made over the twenty dollars you gave him. I was mortified when she handed me back change for my *credit*.' She ducked her head. 'I appreciate your charity, but…'

Vance waited for her to continue, but Stormy seemed to have trouble forming the words. As for himself, he didn't know what to say. He had supposedly set up a small account for Stormy. She wasn't to know the truth about not having to repay the money until long after he was gone from Wayward.

'It's not that I don't…' Stormy struggled with the words, 'don't appreciate your help, Mr Jardeen,' Stormy sounded hesitant. 'I do. I know I would have died without your care. That's a debt I can never hope to repay. But please don't make me more indebted to you. Earning thirty cents a day, I can't hope to pay you back your money before you finish your business at the Indian camp.'

'I never intended you should pay the money back,' Vance replied. 'I arranged the credit idea with the storekeeper. I knew you were too proud to take any charity, but there are times in a person's life when they need a helping hand. I earn a good wage working for the government. I can afford to give a few dollars to a worthy cause.'

'That's what I am to you?' she asked. 'A worthy cause?'

He replied without thinking.

'Yes, Stormy. I think you are about the

most worthy cause I've ever come across in my whole life.'

The statement seemed to suck the draft out of her sails. She fell silent again and kept her eyes to the front.

Vance felt uncomfortable. It was bad enough that his plan at the store had gone askew, but he had also told Stormy she was important to him. What if she misunderstood his intentions? What if she thought he was being generous only in order to take advantage of her?

Jardeen, old buddy, he thought to himself, *when it comes to women, you're about as smooth as sandpaper and as subtle as a Texas tornado!*

CHAPTER SIX

The old Indian chief approached the work detail with a mixture of caution and suspicion. His chin still had a proud lift, but his shoulders were bowed and his face was as wrinkled as a sun-parched prune. The man no longer resembled a war chief of the Sioux. He was a tottery old man with white hair, wearing garments that were worn and tattered with age. Even the burning flames of defiance had died within his once fiery eyes.

Captain Buckley sat erect upon his horse and glared at Yellow Hand. The troopers had planted posts and were beginning to string the spools of barbed wire. Buckley felt a smug satisfaction over the idea of having the Indians securely locked away.

The old chief waved a weathered hand at the new fence.

'What is this new wire, with sharp points like the end of a knife, Soldier Buckley?'

'It's called barbed wire – devil's rope to some,' Buckley replied. 'It's to make sure you and your people damn well stay put. Your slaughter of innocent travelers and settlers has come to an end. This fence will keep you and your pack of wild dogs contained until we are ready to move you to a reservation.'

Yellow Hand gave a sad shake of his head.

'My warriors are all dead or have gone from this place. My people are old men and squaws with children. We are harmless.'

'You weren't harmless, a couple years back, when you attacked an escorted wagon near Cheyenne!' Buckley seethed. 'When you raped and killed a young, beautiful woman and murdered her little six-year-old boy, you sure weren't a bunch of old men and squaws with children! I swore to one day watch you squirm and die, Yellow Hand – you and every last one of your band of butchers!'

'Your soldiers have also killed many of my people, Soldier Buckley. Now, the war is over. You have won. The fighting is done. I wish no more killing.'

'No more killing?' Buckley scoffed. 'After you and your warriors rode with Sitting Bull and massacred Custer's Seventh Cavalry at the Little Big Horn! Now you want *no more killing?*'

'All is in the past,' the chief maintained. 'My people wish only to be left alone.'

'I'll leave you alone, Yellow Hand,' Buckley said vehemently. 'In fact, that's why I'm having this fence built. It's to see that you don't have to worry about anyone entering or leaving your camp.'

'These words are strange to me. Surrounding us with a fence of wire that stabs and cuts – what does it really mean?'

'Just what I said. Your days of killing innocent settlers, then running and hiding are over. If I had my way, this would be your final resting place, Yellow Hand.'

'We were promised another place, a reservation where we can hunt and fish,' the old chief said.

Buckley shook his head.

'I know what you were promised, Yellow Hand. But who can be certain of what the future holds for the killer of women and babies? Perhaps this place will be your Little Big Horn.'

Yellow Hand stared at the fence. He still had puzzlement in his eyes, but Buckley didn't stick around. If he was to dwell upon the loss of his wife and child, he might pull his gun and start shooting. The internal agony was great, the demand for justice overwhelming. He had to ride away, right now, before he lost control and killed the man responsible for their deaths.

Yellow Hand stared after Buckley in wonder. He remembered the event the captain had mentioned. They had attacked the escorted wagon, expecting to find it carrying a stash of guns and ammunition. Instead, it had only some clothes and the mother and son he spoke of. It was many months before he learned that the woman and boy were the family of Captain Buckley. It had not been a fruitful attack, but he could not undo what he and his braves had done. Besides which, they had been at war. They killed every white person they could. That was the meaning of war.

Sergeant Egan, who often brought supplies into the camp, was supervising the building of the fence. He paused to stare at Yellow Hand with a glowing hatred. The chief thought that was odd, for he had shown no such loathing before.

'Are the words true?' Yellow Hand asked the man. 'Will this be our final place? Are we to die here?'

Egan answered brusquely. 'When Captain Buckley was assigned to Wyoming, he was on your side, Yellow Hand. He wanted fair treatment for the Indians, compensation for the slaughter of the buffalo and loss of your hunting grounds. He was an ally – until you murdered his wife and child.'

'It was a time of war,'Yellow Hand replied.

Sergeant Egan spat into the dust. 'You earned his wrath, old man. One day soon you will feel it, and it will be more terrible than anything you ever imagined.'

'This is how the white man treats his prisoners?'

'And how do the Sioux treat their prisoners?' he shot back. 'Other than a few hostages or slaves, your people never took prisoners! You butchered them all on the spot!'

The old chief couldn't argue that point, for the Sioux were practical about the effort required to feed and house prisoners. When raiding with a war party, it was much easier to be rid of any prisoners at the outset.

'I understand Soldier Buckley's hate.'

'You earned it, Yellow Hand,' the sergeant replied. 'Whatever happens to you, know that you earned it.'

With the sloping shoulders of a man who had suffered total defeat, Yellow Hand shuffled off to the cluster of tepees. He had learned little about the fence, but he now felt a new fear, a foreboding of something terrible to come.

Sunday arrived and Vance wandered over to the meeting house to see if Stormy would come to town for the church services. He had not gone far when he caught sight of her. She was just entering town. However, she hadn't come in with the Markley family – her escort was Corporal Dowd! The two of them were in a small, one-horse carriage, with Stormy seated at the corporal's side!

Vance recalled how the man had asked about Stormy and their relationship. He had told him he had no claim on the young woman; she was free to choose her suitors – and she had chosen Dowd!

Vance had intended to try and sit with her for the Sunday meeting, but now... He decided the religious gathering was not in his best interest. He did not like the prospect of sitting back and watching Stormy and Dowd together, talking, laughing, possibly even holding hands during the service!

He turned quickly away, about the time Stormy glanced his way. Rather than wave or nod in her direction, he pretended not to see her. A sudden fire burned in his gut and a scorching envy raked his chest. Damn! it hurt like the devil to see her with another man.

Striding purposefully down the street, he wished the saloon was open. He seldom took a drink of hard liquor, but he felt need of a crutch at the moment. In fact, he rather fancied the idea of drinking himself into a stupor!

Rationality seeped into his thinking process. What was the matter with him? Why did it upset him so at seeing Stormy with another man? He had no claim on her. Wasn't it his intention to finish his job with the Indians and then return to Denver? It should make no difference that she had taken up with Dowd. He seemed like a nice enough guy. Vance ought to have been gratified that Stormy was being courted.

'Dad gum! You're clover-green jealous!' Vance surmised aloud. 'It's the only possible answer. You didn't act upon your feelings and now it's too late!'

Big Irish suddenly appeared in front of him on the street. He moved to block Vance's path and there was fire in his eyes.

'A man what starts talking to himself is sure to have a poor audience, Mr Injun-lover.'

Vance glanced around, but it appeared Irish was alone.

'There be a story going round that the

army is protecting you from we cattlemen, Jardeen.' The man continued his taunting. 'Is it a wee babe you are, needing to be comforted in the night?'

Vance discovered a release for his anger. He marched up to within a step of Big Irish and put a sneer on his own lips. 'You're a real big man, when you have three or four friends at your side, Irish. I wonder how big you are all by yourself.'

'I'll not be needing any help, mate,' Irish said. 'I have it in mind to remove your head with one good punch and you will be needing a good doctor to sew it back in place.'

'Give it your best shot, you Irish mutt.'

Vance was ready for the vicious swing. He ducked under the meaty fist and landed a sharp jab to Irish's jaw. The blow straightened the bigger man up, but he was game for a fight. He shook it off and came in swinging.

Vance should have used what boxing skill he had to maneuver, but he was not in the mood. He met the challenge and the two of them went toe to toe.

Irish had close to fifty pounds on Vance and it made a distinct impression, each time he connected with his punches. Vance stood firm and took a fair share of pounding, feeling every single punch. Irish walloped him about his head, then his ribs, then his head again. One particularly hard shot caused him to end up on the ground.

For all of his size and brutality, Big Irish was not a dirty fighter. He stepped back and waited for Vance to get to his feet, before he launched another attack.

During the second round, Vance got a few good licks of his own. Soon both of them were bloodied and bruised. Vance was not yet fully recovered from being dragged, but Irish had been overconfident. He got careless, and when he missed landing a powerful roundhouse right hand it left a brief opening. Vance exploited the opportunity and drove his right fist upward at the man's jaw. When he connected, the force sent a hearty jolt all the way up his shoulder.

The vicious blow sent Irish reeling back on to his heels. Before he could recover, Vance pounded him twice more, hitting him with every ounce of strength he could muster. Irish staggered and tried to maneuver, but his legs were rubbery and uncertain. He sluggishly attempted to maintain his balance, but he was out on his feet. Vance drew back to hit him again, but held up. The fellow's expression was totally blank and his eyes were glassy and unseeing. The big man swayed, like a tree bending with the wind, then he sank to the ground in a heap. The fight was finished.

The knock at the door roused Vance from his lethargy. He sought to get up, but he ached all over and was unable to manage the feat.

'What?' he asked, turning his head toward the door. 'Who is it?'

'It's me,' Stormy's familiar voice replied. 'Can I come in?'

'It isn't proper for a single lady to enter a man's hotel room,' he grumbled. 'Go away and leave me alone.'

But the door opened and Stormy entered the room. She was still wearing her Sunday dress. She took one look at him and groaned her displeasure.

'Not again!'

When he didn't reply, she hurried over to the table and poured some water from the pitcher into a pan. Next, she picked up a towel and gave a shake of her head.

'Someone said you had been fighting with Big Irish again!' she scolded him. 'The man is half again your size. What's the matter with you?'

'I wanted to thank him for the treatment he and his pals gave me on my first day in town.' Vance replied with some pride: 'I'm the one who walked away this time.'

'Yes, and your victory was so complete, you can't even stand up.'

'Maybe,' he admitted, 'but it hurts a whole lot less when you win the fight.'

She set the pan of water down on the stand next to the bed. Vance started to sit up, but she placed a hand on his chest and forced him to lie back. Then she meticulously began to dab the wet towel against his swollen face.

'Does your escort know you're here?' he asked.

'I suppose you are referring to Corporal Dowd.'

'Unless you've traded him in for another beau lately.'

His snide remark initiated a frown of defiance. 'What was I supposed to do?' Stormy asked. 'The corporal asked if he could bring me into town for the Sunday meeting. I didn't have a good excuse not to ride in with him.'

'When did you hear about the fight?' Vance changed the subject.

'The church meeting was barely under

way when a couple of people arrived to tell the story. The corporal and I hurried over to help, but you were already gone and Irish was being loaded into a wagon, so they could take him home.'

'How'd he look?'

'Like he'd been run over by a herd of cattle. He muttered something about needing another few minutes to figure out your fighting style. I don't think he realized the fight was over.'

'I can attest to the fact he has a hard head. I swear, I hit him hard enough a couple of times that it should have knocked him down – along with about three of his relatives!'

'When it comes to hard heads, I doubt his skull is any thicker than yours,' she said pointedly. 'Was your strategy to block all of his punches with your face?'

Vance flinched when Stormy touched a sore spot above his eye. She had a very gentle hand, as if she were treating her own child, but even that hurt at the moment.

'How long will you continue to risk your life in Wayward?' she asked.

'I'll be ready to start my work at the Indian camp tomorrow or the next day. With any luck, I should be done in a week or so. Once that's finished, I only have to telegraph the War Department and they will send troops to move the Indians.'

'Corporal Dowd said they were putting a barbed-wire fence around the encampment. Why would they do that, if you are going to be done so soon?'

Vance frowned – wincing at the pain the expression caused.

'A fence?' he asked, curious at the statement.

'That's what he said.'

'Where is the good corporal?'

'I asked him to wait downstairs.'

'Good idea,' Vance said drily, 'it wouldn't do to have two roosters crowing on the same fence.'

'What is that supposed to mean?' Stormy displayed an instant irritability. 'You've made it clear from the start that you are only here to do a job. Then you will be leaving.'

'Well, maybe I shouldn't have...' Vance started to say but she didn't allow him to go further.

'Nothing has been said between us.' Her tone grew more harsh and critical. 'You've not made a single overture toward me which might be construed as romantic. I have to assume that I mean nothing to you. And once your job is completed, you are going to ride away and never look back.'

'I guess it might seem that way, but–'

'How else should it seem! If you had any feelings for me you should have been man enough to speak up. You're the one who put me in this awkward position in the first place.'

'Dad gum, Stormy, I didn't know if you – how you would–'

'For heaven's sake!' She was becoming more irate with each passing second. 'You can't be afraid to talk openly to me! We ate and lived together for nearly two weeks. When I was in need of aid and comfort, we even shared the same bed!'

Her heated declaration had barely escaped her lips when Corporal Dowd unexpectedly appeared in the doorway. The shock of over-hearing her bizarre confession caused him to display a mystified expression. However, he immediately put his attention on Vance and neither commented on nor questioned her remark.

'Big Irish is outside on the street, Mr Jardeen,' Dowd said guardedly. 'He says he would like to have a word with you. I'm not sure what he wants, but I don't think it's another fight.'

It took all of the strength Vance could

muster, but he managed to sit up and swing his legs over the side of the bed.

'Thanks, Corporal,' he said. 'I'll be right out.'

Dowd gave a bob of his head and left. Vance glanced at Stormy and saw her cheeks were flushed with shame. There could be no doubt the trooper had overheard her declaration about how they had shared the back of the wagon during her illness.

'There goes my reputation,' she murmured. 'I had to blurt out that we have slept together.'

'It won't make me look any bigger in the Corporal's eyes either,' Vance said. 'No honorable or decent man sleeps with a woman without asking her to be his wife.'

'For a man, to bed a woman is a conquest,' she argued. 'It's the woman who is disgraced.'

'I did mention the words *honorable* and *decent*.' he countered. 'Besides, I can take Dowd aside and explain what you meant. I'm sure we can trust him to keep quiet about your bout with smallpox.'

'You needn't explain anything to anyone on my behalf, Mr Jardeen,' she replied, oozing with a cool vexation. 'I am perfectly able to take care of myself.'

Vance wished he knew what to say, a way to clear the air between them, but this was not the time. Big Irish was waiting. With any luck, the big man would shoot and kill him in the next five minutes. Then, at least, he would be out of his misery.

CHAPTER SEVEN

Big Irish held his hat in his hands. One eye was swollen closed and he had other scrapes and bruises showing on his face. He waited until Vance came out of the building before he lifted his head to speak.

'I come here to make peace with you, Mr Jardeen,' he began. 'Any man who can best me in a fight sure enough deserves me respect. I'll be saying there are no hard feelings betwixt you and me – far as I'm concerned.'

Vance flexed his shoulders and grimaced.

'There may be peace between us, but I'm still suffering some hard feelings. You pack a real punch.'

'Ay,' Irish replied, 'I've had me share of physical disputes before. But I'm admitting, I've never been knocked off me stool the way you done.' He stuck out his hand. 'I come here to assure you I won't be giving you no more trouble. That goes for me friends too.'

Vance stepped forward to take his offered hand and they exchanged a firm grip. Then

Irish backed up and placed his hat on his head.

'I've had me say.'

'I appreciate your stopping by, Big Irish,' Vance said. 'I much prefer a man like you as an ally to an enemy.'

'You need any help with them red devils – anything at all – you only have to give out a holler. You can number Big Irish and his mates among your allies.'

'Thanks, Irish,' Vance was sincere. 'That means a lot to me.'

The large brute turned about and walked away, Stormy had come out behind Vance. She moved over to the corporal and looked him square in the eye.

'Mr Dowd, now that these two barbarians have formed an alliance and made Wayward a haven of peace and good will, I would very much appreciate a ride home.'

'Certainly, Miss Malone,' the corporal responded quickly. 'I'll get the carriage and be right back.'

As he hurried off, Stormy cast an icy stare at Vance.

'Mr Jardeen, I hope you have no more trouble concerning the disposition of the Indians.' Her voice softened a bit, but a flinty spark remained in her gaze. 'If I don't see you again, I shall always be indebted to you for helping me survive my illness.'

'You were there for me after I got roughed up,' Vance replied. 'I'd say we're square on that count.'

Then the two of them stood in an awkward silence. Vance racked his brain, seeking the correct words which would melt the icy wall between them. However, Corporal Dowd was quick to return and the opportunity was lost.

'Good day to you, Mr Jardeen,' Stormy said with a distinct finality. 'I wish you the best of luck.'

Vance managed a nod and watched, helpless, numb and powerless, as she climbed aboard the carriage. He maintained an outward calm, but inside it felt as if a dust devil was trapped within his chest. The swirl of emotion and ache was worse than the bruises from his brawl with Big Irish. He watched as Corporal Dowd guided the horse and carriage out of town, toward the Markley house.

'Jardeen, old boy,' he muttered to himself, 'if living was one big poker-game, I'd say you just lost the biggest hand of your life.'

Captain Buckley looked over the barbed

wire fence with a sense of satisfaction. Working in shifts, his men had completed the encirclement of the Indian camp in two days. The only gate was at the top of the hill, and he had guards posted there to keep watch.

'The animals are caged good and proper.' Sergeant Egan spoke at his side. 'As per your orders, I have two patrols out at all times, watching the camp day and night. Yellow Hand and his braves are not going anywhere.'

'I'm thinking of recalling Corporal Dowd from town,' Buckley informed his friend. 'The corporal should be the one in charge of dealing with the Indians. He can be the one to pass along any future goods or information to Yellow Hand and his people.'

'Good thinking, Cap.'

Buckley expelled a long sigh.

'I've waited a long time to get control of Yellow Hand and his butchers. A long, long time.'

'I remember,' Egan said quietly. 'I was at your side when we buried your wife and little boy. Those buzzards deserve nothing but utter contempt and a slow death.'

Buckley grunted his agreement.

'Before they slink off to a safe haven to

indulge in songs and stories of their great victories over the white man, maybe that's exactly what they will get.'

'What are your orders?'

'Is there any word on when the Indian Affairs man is going to get started? We could stand to know when processing is to begin.'

'Corporal Dowd reported that Jardeen and Big Irish squared off for a second time Sunday morning,' answered Egan. 'Irish had to be carried away.'

'And Jardeen?'

'Dowd said the Indian agent fared much better the second go around. However, I doubt he will be ready to make the ride out here for another day or two.'

'Perhaps I misjudged him,' Buckley admitted. 'I didn't figure him to be that hardy. Big Irish is a tall hill to climb over. After taking a beating that first day, when he was dragged out of town, to come back swinging and win a fight with Irish – the guy must be a tough *hombre*.'

'I'm inclined to agree, Cap.'

'I want you to ride in to Wayward and check on Mr Jardeen; get a feel for when he will be ready to start working with the Indians.'

'OK, Cap, I'll speak to him. You can count on me.'

'If it appears it is safe for Jardeen to manage his own affairs, you can send the corporal and his two comrades back here. As I told you, we need Dowd ready to stand by for any exchange with Yellow Hand's people.'

'Will do, Cap.'

Buckley nodded. 'You are the one man I trust completely, Sergeant Egan. When this is over, I'll see about getting you that next stripe.'

Egan grinned. 'Probably be too heavy on my sleeves.'

'See you when you return,' Buckley said.

'With any luck, I'll be back by late tonight, Cap.' Sergeant Egan raised his hand in a respectful salute.

'So long, Sergeant. Be careful.'

Egan went off to get his horse and Buckley rubbed his hands together. The time was getting close. Every aspect of his plan would soon come together. Before long, he would be rid of this disagreeable duty. He would be back to being a soldier, not a nursemaid for a bunch of reservation-bound barbarians.

Vance was using a curry comb on his horse when the sergeant arrived. He broke off from the chore and stepped over to meet him.

Sergeant Egan dismounted and used his

hand to brush the dust off his shirt.

'We could do with some rain,' he began. 'It's as dry as a mummy's coffin lately.'

'I've never seen a mummy,' Vance said. 'Read about one once.'

'The captain sent me to fetch our men,' Egan explained. Then showing a grin, 'That is, unless you have managed to make a host of other enemies around town.'

'I believe the harassment is over.'

'The captain also wanted to know when we might expect you at the Indian encampment. We've had concerns about some of Yellow Hand's braves sneaking out at nights.'

'They get into any mischief?'

'Not to my knowledge,' Egan replied. 'But there have been some reports of thefts and vandalism and the like. To remedy the situation, we constructed a fence around the Indian camp. The captain wanted me to assure you that we'll have every last one of those savages ready for your count and inventory.'

'I'm sorry to put the captain to the extra trouble. Had I not been laid up these last few days, there would have been no need to build any fence.'

'I hear you had a second run-in with one

of the local bullies.'

'We came to terms.'

The sergeant grinned again, taking a closer look at the bruises on Vance's face.

'Looks as if those were some pretty hard terms.'

Vance stuck to business.

'The dizziness has pretty much cleared up. I'll be heading out to Camp Sage to get started tomorrow. If Yellow Hand and his people co-operate, the job shouldn't take but a few days.'

'Don't push it too soon, or you might end up back in bed,' advised Egan.

'I'm feeling pretty good,' Vance replied. 'I'll be OK.'

'Then we'll expect to see you tomorrow afternoon, Jardeen. Give my best to your lady friend.'

Vance didn't bother telling him how he and the lady weren't exactly on the best of terms. It was not the sergeant's business.

Egan took the reins of his horse and started walking up the street. Vance was relieved the man hadn't made a fuss. Some military men hated the chore of watching and tending prisoners. There had been added work to the task by having to erect a fence. If he had not encountered Stormy and her family, he would have been finished with his job and the Indians would be half-way to the reservation by this time. Had he gone directly to Camp Sage and had the soldiers arrange escort for Stormy to come to town, he would have most of the Indians listed and ready for transport. His concern for Stormy had changed everything.

The ache crept into his chest again. Every time he allowed the woman to enter his thoughts, he was struck with the same empty feeling, a lost and hopeless sensation. He didn't know what it meant, but he didn't like it one bit.

Vance returned to currying his horse. He had him back in the corral, when the corporal and the other two soldiers stopped by.

'Guess the captain thinks you're out of the woods – troublewise.' Dowd winked. 'If you would have whipped Big Irish the first go around, we likely wouldn't have been assigned to keep an eye on you.'

'The idea occurred to me at the time,' Vance replied to the taunt. 'It was the other three men joining in against me who threw a road-apple into the pudding.'

Corporal Dowd chuckled.

'That's pretty lame excuse, Jardeen.'

'You fellows heading back to the fort?'

Vance changed the subject.

'Sergeant Egan gave the order a few minutes ago.' Dowd uttered a sigh. 'Guess that means I won't be around to escort Miss Malone to the Markley place when she gets off work tonight. Would you pass along my apologies?'

'I'll tell her,' Vance promised, suddenly feeling better. 'Don't worry about it.'

'Thanks, Jardeen,' Dowd said. 'See you out at the fort.'

'Probably tomorrow,' Vance told him.

The corporal raised a hand in valediction and the three troopers rode away. Vance appreciated that they had been there to keep the peace, but he was glad to see them go. Stormy now faced the choice of riding with him or making the long walk to the Markely place. He was reasonably certain she would accept his offer. Here was the chance he needed to clear the air between them.

Colonel Voight looked as shocked as if someone had dumped hot ashes into his drawers. His eyes grew wide and he slammed his fist into the palm of his hand.

'Smallpox!' he cried. 'How is that possible? We confined the wagons and the infected people! They were all quarantined! No one has entered the valley since the disease broke out. How did this happen?'

Buckley heaved a great sigh. 'We believe a couple of Indians slipped over to the wagon train and stole some blankets and goods. Those thieving coyotes took the infection right back to camp with them.'

'Are any of our men down sick?' the colonel asked, dread and worry naked in his expression. 'Have we all been exposed?'

'I believe we're safe, Colonel. My standing orders have been that the men keep a safe distance from Yellow Hand and his tribe. I'm reasonably certain we can contain the outbreak without contaminating our troops.'

The colonel paced once about the room, then stopped and frowned at Buckley.

'I hold you responsible for this, Captain. You were to keep those Indians under constant guard.'

'It's the reason I had the fence installed, Colonel. Once we had to send out men to patrol the border, we simply didn't have the manpower to keep watch over the entire camp twenty-four hours a day. It's obvious that some of Yellow Hand's warriors have been sneaking off at nights and getting into mischief. I'm afraid we got our fence in place too late.'

'This infectious disease must be contained, Captain. I don't want to be forced to issue a quarantine for this entire part of the country.'

'We are taking every precaution, sir. There's no evidence to indicate the disease has spread beyond the Indian camp. As I said, no physical contact with the Indian populace has been made in the past couple weeks. We should be safe.'

'For the sake of us all, I hope you're right about that.'

'What are your orders, sir?' the captain asked.

'Gather any volunteers you can find, those who have already had smallpox and are willing to help out at the Indian camp. Unless those people get help, and get it damn quick, the majority of them are going to perish.'

'Yes, sir,' Buckley said.

The colonel sighed. 'Those poor, ignorant people. They couldn't have known that stealing a few items from the wagon train would mean the death of a good many of their own people. If history is any indication, those Indians will have no immunity. This disease could literally wipe them out to the last man.'

'Like a pack of wild dogs feasting on the corpse of a poisoned lamb,' Buckley stated firmly. 'They have caused their own un-doing. Perhaps God has decreed that they should pay for their grisly crimes!'

The words came out more harshly than Buckley had intended. He was instantly aware of the colonel regarding him with a narrowed gaze.

'I'm mindful of your personal contempt for the Indians, Captain. But let's remember they are human beings – not so different from the rest of us.'

'Of course, sir.'

'Recruit those men who served at the wagon train and enlist the aid of any who might want to volunteer from the train or from Wayward. It's going to take every person we can muster to give those people a fighting chance to survive.'

'Yes, sir. I'll see to it straight away.'

CHAPTER EIGHT

Seeing Stormy home failed to be the opportunity Vance had intended. Stormy accepted the ride, but she was taciturn and withdrawn. As for Vance, he had rehearsed what he wanted to say a dozen times, but the words sounded ridiculous to him now. By the time he eventually reined up in front of the Markley house, he was desperate.

'How are you holding up?' he asked. 'It must be tough on you, doing such hard work and being on your feet all day.'

'I'll manage,' Stormy said simply.

Vance's thoughts were about as confused and muddled as a freshly stirred puddle. He couldn't get his brain to function. This might be the last time he was alone with Stormy. He had to find the courage to say what he felt.

'Are you going to help me down?' she asked, obviously growing tired of waiting.

'Yes, ma'am,' were the only words to surface.

He dismounted and then reached up for

her, placing his hands at Stormy's waist. She leaned toward him and slid gracefully off the horse. He set her down, but, rather than let go, he continued to hold her close to him.

'I can stand under my own power,' Stormy said, mindful of his hesitation to let go. 'I'm not so frail you have to support me.'

'No, ma'am,' Vance said, quickly withdrawing his hands. He took a step back and ducked his head. 'Sorry about that.'

A frown wrinkled Stormy's brow. 'Why are you suddenly calling me ma'am again?'

'Excuse me?'

'After what we've been through together, we are more than mere acquaintances.'

Vance took a deep breath and summoned his last ounce of resolve. Here it went – come hell or a slap across the face! He was going to speak his piece!

But the sound of a running horse turned their attention to the main trail. It was Sergeant Egan, and he had his sights set on them both. He guided his horse up to them and jerked him to a halt.

'Found you!' he exclaimed, directing his attention to Vance. 'I was afraid I'd have to look all over town.'

'What's the matter, Sergeant?' Vance asked.

Egan shook his head solemnly.

'There's trouble at Camp Sage, Jardeen. The captain thought you ought to be informed at once.'

'What kind of trouble?' Vance was immediately concerned.

'First off, didn't you mention that you had once had smallpox?'

'That's right.'

'Well, the colonel is asking for volunteers to work at the Indian encampment.'

Vance caught his breath.

'The Indian camp?' he repeated. 'What for?'

'Smallpox,' the sergeant announced. 'It appears the Indians have contracted the disease.'

Vance felt his stomach roll over at the news.

'Are you saying the epidemic wasn't kept in check?'

'We believe a couple of Indians sneaked over to loot the diseased wagons and stole infected goods. They are spreading smallpox throughout the entire tribe. A fair number of them are sick with signs of the disease. We've only got a half-dozen troopers who can help and there are nearly a hundred women and children in their camp. Plus, our men are already exhausted from tending folks over at the wagon train for the past few weeks. We're looking for anyone who has a mind to help.'

'I can help,' Stormy spoke up. 'I've already had the disease.'

Egan appeared surprised at the news. Vance figured someone at the wagon train might have mentioned the family that had been left behind. However, it made little difference now. The plague was alive and seeking new victims – Indian victims, a people with little or no immunity to the wretched pestilence.

'I'll head up there first thing in the morning,' Vance said.

'I'm coming too,' Stormy insisted. 'I'll do what I can to help.'

'That's very Christian of you, ma'am,' Egan said. Then, turning his attention to Vance again, 'I wonder if you wouldn't mind asking around town for help? There might be a few folks who have had smallpox living in Wayward. Maybe some of them would be willing to help too.'

'I can ask, but the Indians aren't real popular hereabout.'

The sergeant bobbed his head up and down.

'Yeah, I know, Jardeen, but it's worth a shot.'

'How many volunteers do you have so far?' asked Vance.

'Just our half-dozen troopers and three civilians from the wagon train. Not nearly enough to handle an epidemic.'

'I agree,' Vance said.

'Report to me or Captain Buckley, out at the post, Jardeen. I've got to gather up some supplies and round up some medicine for fighting the fever. I'll be back out at Camp Sage when you arrive.'

As soon as the sergeant had ridden away, Vance turned and looked at Stormy. She was unable to hide the feeling of dread and fear.

'They claim it never strikes the same person twice,' he attempted to reassure her.

'I'm more concerned with being strong enough to deal with the suffering and death. I-I hope I can....' But her voice cracked with emotion. After a little while she recovered enough to continue. 'I only wish to be of some help,' she finished.

'I'll stop by the laundry and tell your lady boss the news. Come daylight, I'll be here to pick you up.'

'I'll be ready.'

135

Vance still wished for the chance to speak his mind, but this was not the time. The pitiful attempt of a lovelorn dunce confessing his feelings was a trifle when compared to a hundred people being infected with smallpox. The baring of his soul would have to wait.

Vance made the rounds to just about every business establishment in Wayward and had no success. He eventually entered the saloon and met up with Big Irish. The rancher was playing cards, but left the table when he spied Vance. He threaded his way past the other tables and gave a shake of his head.

''Tis a sorry-looking mutt you be this night, mate,' he greeted Vance. 'There be a rumor by some who say the plague has struck the Indian camp.'

'I'm afraid it's no rumor,' Vance replied. 'I've been asking for help from anyone who has already had the disease. We need volunteers.'

'Can't say I've had the pleasure,' Irish replied. 'Is it looking to save them red-hides you are?'

'There are a lot of women and children in the camp.'

'Ay,' Irish displayed a serious expression.

'I've nothing against the helpless and them who never done any harm.' Then with a colder tone of voice, 'But – may the saints forgive me – I wouldn't shed me a tear if every one of Yellow Hand's murdering braves should wither and die.'

Vance ignored his sentiment. 'Do you know of any ranch hands or men around who have survived an attack of smallpox?'

'I'm thinking I don't know of a soul, Jardeen, and that's the truth.'

'We might need some other kinds of help down the road. Can I count on you?'

The man grinned. 'Whatever you need, Indian-lover. Big Irish and me mates would be only too happy to oblige.'

Vance tipped his head in acknowledgment.

'See you later.'

'Ay, if you don't die of the disease or from a red-hide knife in your back.'

The search for help was fruitless. If any of the town's people had suffered through smallpox, they weren't of a mind to volunteer. After living through it himself, then treating Stormy and her relatives, Vance could not blame them. Smallpox was probably as ugly and horrible as any disease on earth. No one who witnessed it close up would ever want to be around it a second time.

It was a solemn trip out to Camp Sage. Stormy, except for thanking Vance for acquiring a carriage, hardly said a word during the four-hour ride. When they neared the fort, a young officer came out to greet them.

'Lieutenant Gordon, at your service,' he stated professionally. 'You and the lady...' he looked past them down the road. 'Is that the total sum of the help we can expect from Wayward?'

'I'm afraid so,' Vance replied. 'I'm Vance Jardeen, sent here by the War Department, and this is Miss Malone. She's the one and only volunteer from Wayward.'

'The confinement of those Indians was the army's responsibility,' the lieutenant admitted ruefully. 'I don't know how they managed to sneak over to the infected wagon train. Our patrols were on constant guard, over both the Indians and the wagons.'

'Some say an Indian can move without making a sound,' Vance said. 'Plus, you had no way of knowing some of the braves would venture off and steal from the wagon train.'

'There aren't but a few able-bodied men

in the Indian camp. Most of Yellow Hand's fighting men deserted or were killed before their surrender. The tribe is made up mostly of women, children and a few old men.'

'From the way Captain Buckley spoke, I thought of them as practically being ready to hit the warpath,' Vance said.

'The good captain is unduly sensitive when it comes to Yellow Hand. The chief and his followers were responsible for killing his wife and child some years back.'

Vance absorbed the information.

'I didn't know.'

'Yes, Jardeen. He's a darned good officer, but his hatred of Indians sometimes borders on madness.'

'Is he still in charge of the camp?' Vance asked.

The lieutenant nodded his head.

'For the present. And, I suspect, he is likely celebrating this tragic turn of events. I'm sure he feels Yellow Hand deserves this epidemic.'

'We are here to do what we can to help, though I doubt it will be much.'

'It's good of you both to offer,' the lieutenant replied. 'If you'll follow me, I'll have someone take charge of your carriage and horse.'

Vance waved him ahead and they followed along after the officer and his horse.

'About now,' Vance mused to Stormy, 'I'm wishing I'd taken the job of managing the War Department's office in Denver.'

'I can't believe you'd want to miss out on all of this fun,' said Stormy, drily.

'Yeah,' Vance attempted a lightness in his voice. 'I don't know what I was thinking.'

Within minutes, they had been provided with blankets and towels. When they reached the gate to the fenced compound, Corporal Dowd was there to greet them.

'I wish I could say it was nice to see you again, Miss Malone,' he said to Stormy, then quickly stepped over to take the items she had been carrying. 'I'm sorry you have to be a part of this nightmare.'

'How bad is it?' Vance asked. 'Beginning stages or worse?'

'It hit them like a herd of stampeding buffalo, Jardeen. These people don't seem to have any resistance at all.'

'How many are infected?'

'Practically every man, woman and child are down sick or showing signs of the disease. It's going to be real bad for the next few days.'

'Where do we bunk?'

'We erected a tent next to the critical station, kind of made it our hospital,' Dowd explained. 'We can move some of the worst cases to the station. It's nearest to the gate and our water supply. Also, it's where the funeral wagon will pick up and haul away the dead. The men have dug a pit a hundred yards from camp for burning the bodies.'

They went into the shelter and tossed their things on the ground. There was no time to make up beds or get organized. The need was too great.

Smallpox had decimated the Indian camp. As Dowd had warned, the pestilence had infected nearly everyone. By the end of the first week, the dead were piled up at the hospital station, stacked like cordwood for the burial detail. The fire burning beyond the camp roared day and night, endlessly consuming the remains of the deceased.

Vance and the others worked around the clock, attempting to force water down swollen throats and laboring to make the victims comfortable. Their efforts were futile, for the Indians had no resistance to the disease. Many of those struck down died within a few days. Even the strongest of their number succumbed to the deadly disease.

The worst job was tending the sick children. Vance and Stormy battled the hardest when trying to save the young lives. However, the victories were few. Most often, they could only watch the suffering and swallow the regret of defeat. The disease extracted a heavy toll, killing nine out of every ten victims.

Days and nights commingled together. The hours of rest were few and the pain and misery was great. Stormy held up as well as Vance, until the eighth day. Vance was carrying buckets of fresh water and spied her a few feet inside the critical station tent. She was cradling the lifeless body of an infant, resting on her knees and rocking back and forth. The glassy stare in her eyes told him she had reached a point of mental and physical exhaustion. He set down his buckets and moved over to kneel down at her side.

'It's OK,' he whispered to her. A quick examination revealed the tiny body was cold. The child was lost.

'I'll take her,' he said carefully. Then he removed the baby from her arms and placed the child onto a nearby cot. Stormy remained on the ground, staring blankly off into space. Vance scooped her up in his arms and carried her the short way to their own tent.

When he laid her down on her bed,

Stormy rolled onto her stomach and began to weep into the blankets. Vance stayed at her side and gently massaged her about the back, neck and shoulders.

'You shouldn't have come,' he told her softly. 'Surrounded by all this death and horror, it's more than a person can stand. Especially so soon after your own bout with smallpox. It's only been a couple weeks since you were lying in bed, in not much better shape than many of these people. I'll speak to Dowd and have them take you back to town.'

'No! I can't go,' she sobbed. 'The children, the babies – they're dying, and there's no one else to hold them and offer comfort. I can't leave!'

He lowered his head.

'I know how you feel, Stormy, but it's a hopeless situation now. There aren't more than a handful who are going to survive.'

She sniffed back her tears.

'Have you seen any here who aren't afflicted?' she asked.

'Nary a one. The pestilence struck down every last one in the camp.'

'And we're helpless,' Stormy murmured. 'We can do nothing but sit by and watch the children die.'

'Try and get a few hours of rest,' he coaxed. 'You've been up for two days straight. You need to get some sleep.'

She turned on to her back and closed her eyes, but rolled her head side to side. 'I pray I don't dream. The dreadful images of...' She didn't have to finish.

Vance covered her with a blanket and tucked it up around her shoulders. He paused to brush the hair back from her face and then leaned down and kissed her on the forehead. The action caused her brown eyes to flicker open.

'I haven't been tucked in since I was a child,' she murmured.

'Get some sleep,' he said. 'I'll stay with you for a little while.'

Her eyes closed once more and, within a few minutes, her even breathing revealed she had succumbed to a fatigued slumber.

Vance watched her for a short while, then spread a blanket on the ground next to her. His own energy was spent. He needed to catch a little sleep too. Considering how little they could do to help the stricken population, it was unlikely a few hours would make much difference.

CHAPTER NINE

Something disturbed Vance's sleep. He came awake to discover Stormy was preparing breakfast. He blinked against the morning's light and stretched.

'You up already?' Vance asked.

'I feel guilty stopping to eat or sleep, even though I know it's necessary.'

Vance rubbed his chin and realized he had several days' growth of whiskers. His clothes were also dirty and soiled from treating the sick. Stormy was not much better off, but watching her still caused his heart to beat more rapidly.

'How much longer before this dreadful siege is over?' Stormy asked.

Vance shook his head, weary of the hopeless battle.

'I'd guess several more days. By then, the few who are still hanging on will either get well or die. From the looks of it, I won't have but a handful of people to process for the reservation.'

Stormy sighed. 'It's appalling. Out of more

than a hundred, only a dozen or so will survive. I can't imagine a more horrible disease than smallpox.'

'I spoke to Yellow Hand.' Vance changed the subject. 'He speaks passable English. He told me none of his people had stolen anything from the infected wagon train.'

'Do you think he would admit it if they did?'

'I don't know,' Vance said. 'How many actual warriors have you tended?'

'Maybe one or two,' Stormy replied. 'The male Indians in this camp are mostly elderly men or children.

'Captain Buckley spoke as if this was a tribe of warriors, ready to sweep out over the countryside and massacre every white person they could find.'

Stormy scoffed at the idea.

'Yellow Hand might have once been a leader of a war party, but he's only a poor, tired, old man now.'

'Something else strikes me as odd,' Vance said. 'Of all the Indian tepees I've been inside, I've not seen anything from the wagon train except for a couple homemade quilts and blankets.'

'Why would they only steal blankets?' Stormy asked. 'Isn't the army responsible for supplying all of the bedding the Indians required?'

'This was a temporary camp. I suppose they might have run short on supplies to feed and handle the Indians.'

'So a couple of the Indians sneaked over to the quarantined wagon train and stole infected blankets?'

Vance shrugged. 'It's a possibility, but why didn't they steal anything else? There are no guns or horses in this camp. A Plains Indian is nothing without a horse. It's OK for the women and children to walk, but a warrior travels on horseback. If they were going to steal from the wagon train, they would have targeted the riding-stock and weapons.'

'Maybe the warriors did steal horses and therefore they did not return to the camp. They would know they couldn't expect to hide those horses in the Indian camp.'

'But the blankets are here. That means they did return from the theft.' Vance groaned at the puzzlement. 'Nothing about this makes sense.'

Stormy served him up a plate of hot beans, mixed with a portion of salt pork. The coffee was strong enough to have stood firm without a cup, but it was all they had.

The meal was eaten in silence. To speak

was to disturb the deathly stillness which surrounded the entire camp. Many of the tents were empty now, their occupants having been victims of the plague. The number of surviving Indians had dwindled each day until few were left alive. It was a camp of horror and gloom.

'We'd better finish up and get back to the sick.' Stormy spoke first. 'I feel guilty, sitting here and sipping coffee, while so many are suffering.'

Vance bobbed his head in agreement.

'You're right. Just don't try and do too much. I don't want you making yourself sick from working too hard.'

Stormy managed a jaded smile. Even tired, dispirited, with her hair pulled back and in disarray, he thought she was about the most beautiful person on earth.

'Don't worry about me,' she said. 'I'm fine.'

As Stormy walked away, a thousand words were scrambled within Vance's mind. He desperately wanted to convey his feelings to her, to tell her she was more than just a friend. But she disappeared out of their tent, while he remained rooted to the ground like a post.

'Idiot,' he grunted to himself. 'She's going

to be married and have two kids, before you ever find the guts to tell her how you feel!'

Sergeant Egan was haggard and red-eyed from the long hours. He crossed from the checkpoint after a shower and change of clothes. He was dragging from long hours of keeping watch over the Indian camp and supervising the burial detail.

Captain Buckley waited until he came up next to him before speaking.

'What do you have to report, Sergeant?'

'It's like standing in the middle of Custer's final battle, Cap,' replied the sergeant. 'Everywhere you look are bodies. There are moans and groans of the dying all around. I know the disease can't hurt me, but it still scares hell out of me.'

'How about Yellow Hand?' Buckley asked.

'He's down with the pox, but is still hanging on. His daughter and grandson have both died, so he has no family left.'

Buckley sighed deeply.

'Think the old war horse will make it?'

'He is tougher than parched rawhide,' Egan said. 'He might survive, but it looks as if eighty or ninety per cent of his people will perish from the disease.'

'Has anyone been overtly curious as to

how the Indians were infected?' the captain asked.

'Jardeen, the Indian Affairs man, is the only one who seems real curious. He's the one guy who might figure out the truth.'

Buckley rubbed his chin thoughtfully.

'That could be trouble.'

'When he was tending to Yellow Hand, I happened to be close enough to hear him asking the old chief some pointed questions.'

'What kind of questions?'

'He wanted to know about the braves who stole from the wagon train.' Egan shook his head. 'After his chat, he asked me whether the army had provided adequate blankets and food for the Indians. I said we'd given them what extra supplies we had, but he is likely to draw his own conclusions.'

'I don't like the sound of that.'

'He and the Malone woman are the only ones who came in from town,' Egan reported. 'I'm pretty sure we're OK with the volunteers from the wagon train. They don't know squat, and there doesn't seem to be a lot of friendship between them and the Malone woman.'

'Why would that be?'

'Come to find out, Miss Malone and her

aunt and uncle were traveling with the wagon train. Her family was the first to show sign of the pox, so the others on the train abandoned them on the trail.'

Buckley grunted at the news.

'Stupid stunt there. Did they think they could cut and run from something like smallpox?'

'Needless to say, it didn't work. I guess several of them were exposed while they were at Deadwood. By the time they had traveled another twenty miles, the disease had spread throughout the entire train.'

'How about our own snoopy Corporal Dowd? Has he asked any questions?'

'If he has any suspicions, he's keeping them to himself. I don't think he will cause us any trouble on his own. But if he and Jardeen should put their heads together, they might discover those blankets were brought over from the wagon train – by me!'

The captain frowned in thought.

'We can't let that happen, Sergeant. We need to deter Jardeen or the Malone gal from pointing a finger at us.'

'I doubt the woman would make any trouble without him, Cap. And Dowd isn't going to buck your authority because of those red devils.'

'Yes, but what about Jardeen?'

'He could be a problem all right.'

Buckley considered the options for a moment before speaking again.

'I think it would be a good idea if one of Yellow Hand's warriors tried to take vengeance against him.'

Egan was confused. 'Why take a personal vengeance against him?'

'As far as those savages know, this is a white man's disease. A crazed warrior might want to strike back at the first white man he sees.'

Egan let out a deep breath.

'I'm not in favor of killing an innocent man.'

'He wouldn't have to be killed,' Buckley allowed. 'We only need to have him turn his attention to something other than how the Indians contracted smallpox.'

Egan bobbed his head.

'I see what you mean. If he has a close call and thinks one of Yellow Hand's men is out to get him, it will allow us some breathing-room.'

'The alternative could be a court of inquiry and maybe spending our remaining years in a stockade, Sergeant. We need to put him off the scent.'

'I'll give it a shot, Cap, but it's going to be risky. I don't know of a single warrior in camp strong enough to muster any kind of attack. Every grown man is down sick.'

'Do the best you can.'

'I'll give it a go, Cap. You can count on me.'

It was after dark. Vance was about to enter the sleeping-tent when Corporal Dowd tossed the blanket to him. Vance saw the disgust on the man's face and frowned at the colorful quilt.

'What's this?'

'That blanket came from the wagon train. I tended to the elderly woman who had sewn it. Her dying wish was that it be passed on to her daughter.' He shook his head sadly. 'Trouble is, her daughter died the day before she did.'

'What does it mean, Corporal?'

Dowd put his hands on his hips and clenched his teeth.

'I wrapped the woman up in that blanket when I put her body on the disposal wagon. It should have been burned along with her remains!'

Vance let the news sink in.

'Is there any way one of the Indians could

have stolen the blanket before the body reached the fire pit?'

'It sure don't seem likely!' Dowd snapped, growing angry at the obvious conclusion. 'I've gone over it in my head a hundred times. There ain't no way the Indians could have gotten this here quilt into their own camp.'

'Who handled the burial detail?' Vance asked.

'Sergeant Egan. The captain had him in charge of...' Corporal Dowd stopped in mid-sentence and slowly turned his head from side to side in retrospect. 'Thinking back on it, I don't remember him returning after disposing of the load that day.'

'Then it's possible the sergeant brought some contaminated blankets in with the other supplies for the Indians,' Vance speculated.

The corporal swallowed hard, his expression one of pain.

'I couldn't say for certain, Jardeen. I didn't think about it till now. The day after the lady died, I was reassigned to look after you in town.'

'Maybe they wanted you out of the way, so you wouldn't be suspicious.'

'For the love of Jesus, Jardeen! You don't

154

think Sergeant Egan would deliberately infect a bunch of women and children?'

'Captain Buckley seems to hate the Indians with a passion,' Vance said.

'Yes. Yellow Hand was responsible for the death of his wife and child. I suppose it might make him hateful enough to pull a stunt like this.'

'Would Sergeant Egan go along with something so dastardly?'

'The sergeant and the captain have been together for years,' Dowd said. 'Egan was with the captain the day they found the bodies of his wife and son. The tragedy nearly destroyed Buckley, so I've heard.'

'The lieutenant mentioned to me how the man's hate bordered on madness at times,' Vance recalled. 'Is he responsible? Is this his revenge against Yellow Hand for the murder of his wife and child?'

'I hate to admit it, but it could be,' Dowd replied.

Vance uttered a sigh.

'It's getting late. You should get some sleep. As soon as we get the chance, we need to bring this matter before the commander of the post. I don't think the Indians stole any contaminated blankets. I believe they were deliberately infected with smallpox.'

Dowd groaned. 'Buckley has always been a good soldier. He served in the Civil War under General Sherman. He's been decorated several times and turned down a command of his own to remain an active field officer – requesting duty here in Wyoming.'

'And now he has taken his vengeance against Yellow Hand.' Vance shook his head sadly. 'Only Yellow Hand is no longer a dangerous warrior chief. He's an old man, too frail to ride the war path. That's how come he stayed behind, while the other tribes he rode with escaped up into Canada.'

'I reckon so,' the corporal agreed.

'If Buckley conspired with Sergeant Egan to intentionally infect these people, they are guilty of mass murder.'

'We can inform the colonel of what we suspect tomorrow,' Dowd said. 'I sure hate the idea, but there can't be two blankets like that one. I'm afraid the spread of smallpox to the Indians was deliberate.'

'Damn,' Vance murmured, gravely shaking his head. 'There's nothing worse in this world than hate.'

'I agree, Jardeen. Hate and the desire for revenge can turn an otherwise good man into the worst animal alive.' The corporal arched his shoulders to remove some of the ache from the long day's work. 'I've got to inspect the men at the checkpoint. Then I'm turning in for the night.'

'I'm for a little sack time too,' Vance said.

Dowd walked away in the darkness and Jardeen was left standing with the blanket. He was tired and his eyelids were heavy. Stormy had already gone to bed. They had reached a point of exhaustion, where they could do little but watch the dead or dying. The worst part of the wretched chore was the feeling of hopelessness. The treatment they could offer the sick was only to give them water and keep them warm. There was no way to really help them. Smallpox was too deadly. Nothing could slow its dreadful onslaught.

He tucked the blanket under his arm and turned for his tent. Just then, a shadow loomed up in the darkness.

Vance froze for an instant, then glimpsed a flashing blade in the moon's light. It flashed in a deadly arc – directly at his chest!

CHAPTER TEN

Vance reacted instinctively. He dropped the blanket and threw up his hands to protect himself. The arcing knife came down, but he blocked the thrust with his left arm. The blade cut into the flesh, but was instantly withdrawn for a second plunge.

Vance dove at the man's legs and upended him. Before the attacker could recover, Vance caught hold of the man's knife-wielding wrist. They struggled, pitting strength against strength and rolled against the side of a tent. Even as the man sought to pull his wrist free, Vance shifted his weight and swung a doubled fist, striking the man alongside the temple. The blow knocked the man off balance and he lost hold of his knife.

'Help!' Stormy's voice cried out. It had been their tent they had landed against. She had been drawn outside to see what the commotion was all about. 'Someone! Help!' she shouted again.

The cry of alarm caused the assailant to

panic. He struck out with both feet, kicking like a tangled mule. Vance tried to bat aside the vicious flying boots, but one struck him in the chest. It hit him with such force that he could not keep hold of the man. The attacker jumped up and scampered away, weaving a hasty path of retreat through the tepees.

Stormy was at Vance's side, before he could catch his breath or gather wits enough to pursue the man who had attacked him.

'Are you hurt?' her voice sounded frantic. 'Vance? Are you all right?'

He put a hand on her arm to calm her.

'I'm OK,' he told her. 'He came at me with a knife, but he didn't do a lot of damage.'

Dowd had been close enough to hear Stormy's call for help. He came rushing over to the two of them, gun in hand. 'What happened?' he asked, as he searched in the darkness. 'What's going on?'

'Someone dressed like an Indian tried to kill me,' Vance explained, while getting to his feet. 'He dropped his knife and ran.'

Dowd spied the weapon and picked it up to examine it in the moonlight.

'I recall Yellow Hand has a fancy bone-handle knife like this one.'

'The man I tangled with was not Yellow

Hand,' Vance told them both. 'This guy was tough and strong. Besides which, when he kicked me, he was wearing army boots, not moccasins. If Stormy hadn't let out a yell and scared him off, he might have finished me.'

'Why would anyone want you dead?' Dowd asked.

'That's a good question, Corporal.'

'You're bleeding!' Stormy gasped, discovering Vance's sleeve saturated with blood. 'You've been hurt!'

'It was a glancing blow. I don't think it's too bad.'

'Come into the tent,' she said, taking hold of his good right arm. 'Let's get you in where there is some light.'

'I doubt we find that jasper tonight,' Dowd said. 'No telling where he ran off to.'

'You're right, Corporal, he's probably long gone.'

'I'll alert the guards at the gate all the same, then have a look around, Jardeen. You better have Stormy look at that wound. If it looks bad, you should head over to the post and see the surgeon.'

'Thanks, Corporal,' Vance said. 'But I'm sure it's little more than a scratch.'

Dowd uttered a sour grunt. 'I'll look

around and talk to you later. This here detail has gone from bad to worse.'

As Dowd left them, Vance picked up the quilt and then followed Stormy into their tent. The corporal was right, this was not only a dirty chore, it had become a dangerous job as well.

Vance awoke to find the sun was up. He sat up, instantly grimacing at the stab of pain from his injured left arm. There was no need for alarm, though. He discovered Stormy, sitting in front of the door flap, with a rifle across her lap. He had to smile at that, for her chin was resting on her chest. She was sound asleep.

He checked the dressing on his arm, but it was secure. The blood hadn't soaked through the bandage, so he figured the cut was not severe enough to require stitches. He'd been very fortunate.

Moving over to Stormy, Vance removed the rifle from her lap and set it to one side. Then, with the same gentleness he would have used on a child, Vance carried Stormy over to her bed. She almost came awake, but he hushed her softly, telling her to sleep. She obeyed without a fuss, for she was fatigued. Once he assured himself the woman was slumbering peacefully, Vance went out into the morning sun. After a short search, he located Corporal Dowd.

'Have you found anything?' he greeted him.

'I've been up since daylight. The guards are on alert and I made a complete search of the camp.' Dowd uttered a sigh of defeat. 'Yellow Hand's knife was missing, but I didn't find one single brave healthy enough to have attacked you last night, Jardeen. There's only a total of five men alive in camp who are of fighting age. Three are near death and the other two are too sick to stand. Smallpox has taken down every one of them.'

'If that's the case, then we need to look elsewhere.'

Dowd let out a short sigh.

'One thing we know, your attacker wouldn't have risked entering a contaminated camp, not unless he had previously had smallpox. That means it had to be someone like Sergeant Egan.'

Vance frowned. 'Maybe Egan became worried we would figure out he was behind the contaminated blankets?'

'It's a possibility, Jardeen. I think we ought to get word to the colonel right away. He should be made aware of what is going on.'

'Yes, the truth behind the spread of this epidemic is real ugly, Corporal.'

Dowd lowered his head.

'I'm going to head over to the fort and speak to him, Jardeen,' he said quietly. 'I'll tell him about the blanket and also about the attempt on your life last night.'

'All right. I'll take our piece of evidence to the cleansing station and give it a good washing. We'll need it for proof.'

'Good.'

'What do you think the colonel will do?' Jardeen asked.

'I expect he will order the arrest of Sergeant Egan and Captain Buckley. It's unlikely the sergeant would have done this on his own.'

'Once I've thoroughly cleaned the blanket, I'll be along to meet you.'

Dowd hurried off toward the decontamination point where he would wash and change clothes. He had already given the order to have both his and Vance's horses ready to ride. All of the other animals were on a picket line and under guard.

Vance wrapped the incriminating blanket in his poncho and put it with his horse. However, he didn't wish to leave without

163

informing Stormy of what was going on. She would have been confused to wake up and find both him and Dowd gone. He returned to the tent to speak to her.

Stormy was obviously not sleeping soundly. She came awake when he entered.

'What are you doing up so early?' she asked, sitting up. After a short pause to rub the sleep from her eyes, she used a hand to sweep back a lock of hair which was dangling into her face. 'How's your wound?'

'You would make a good nurse,' he said. 'The arm feels good as new.'

'Did the corporal find out anything last night?' she asked.

Vance explained what he and the corporal suspected.

Stormy gave a solemn nod of her head.

'If you're right, the captain's desire for revenge has taken a terrible toll on these people. I realize the death of his wife and child was tragic, as they were innocent victims. But most of these people are innocent victims too. Two wrongs don't make a right.'

Vance stood, awkward and uncomfortable. 'I wanted to let you know what was up before I took my horse and headed over to the cleansing station.'

Stormy lifted her outstretched hands so he could take her by the wrists. He pulled, helping her to her feet. She came up easily, standing but inches away. They had grown dirty and haggard from the long days of tending to the suffering. Stormy's eyes were red from lack of proper rest and her clothes were wrinkled and soiled. Even so, Vance still found her the most beautiful woman he had ever known.

'You've been quite a trooper through all of this, Stormy,' he said.

She managed a tired smile.

'All this time together and this is the first you have noticed that I had some pluck?'

'I guess I'm not the only one who has taken notice of you,' Vance admitted. 'Corporal Dowd has been hot on your heels since he first set eyes on you.'

'Yes,' Stormy replied. 'He asked to court me proper.'

Vance masked the instant dismay and turned away to lead the way out of the tent. It felt as if his heart had sunk to the deepest pit of his stomach. With a mounting dread, and fearful to look at Stormy, he asked:

'What did you tell him?'

There was a slight hesitation before her reply.

'I told him I wanted to wait until this smallpox epidemic was over before making any plans.'

'Good idea,' Vance said, trying to hide his crestfallen condition. 'Emotions always run a little high during a crisis.'

'There have been a dozen other suitors around Wayward asking about me too,' Stormy said matter-of-factly. 'It appears it isn't necessary for me to travel all the way to Utah to find a bounty of potential husbands.'

Walking slowly toward the guard station, Vance suffered a near-panic of trepidation. What if she decided to court Dowd or one of the other men around Wayward? What if he never told her how he felt and she ended up spoken for?

'You got anyone special in mind yet?' he queried, fearful to hear her answer.

Another short pause.

'I'm going to need more time to evaluate the potential suitors. I wouldn't want to make a mistake.'

Vance took a deep breath. He had to get the words out, tell her how he felt. He wanted Stormy to be his woman, to share his life with her. He needed to know where he stood. If he was not her choice, it was best to find out right this minute.

'Stormy, I've been wanting to–'

But his enamored confession was halted before he could finish.

'Vance!' Stormy gasped, pointing at the corral. 'Sergeant Egan! He's stealing your horse!'

Vance swung his attention to the holding-pen and spied Egan. The man was on his own mount, but had also grabbed up the lead rope on Vance's horse. Before he could take a step forward, Egan went out through the gate and rode away at a gallop!

'He must have been watching the camp,' Vance deduced. 'He probably saw Dowd heading over to the post and decided it was too risky for him to go back to the fort. I'll bet he needed an extra horse for his and Buckley's escape.'

'Or he only wanted to slow you down.'

'There's that possibility too.'

'Whatever plan he and Captain Buckley have hatched, it's the army's job now,' Stormy said. 'They will catch them both.'

'With patrols spread out all along the border, and having to watch over these remaining Indians, the fort doesn't have but a handful of men to send after them. Plus, it'll be hours before they get on their trail. If I take one of the horses from the cavvy, I could be after them in fifteen minutes.'

'Why you?' Stormy wanted to know. 'You're not a part of the military. It's not your job to risk your life to catch a couple criminals.'

'I can't let Buckley and Egan get away with infecting and killing all of these Indians. They were supposed to be in the army's care! My care! I was supposed to process these people and have them sent to a reservation, not stand by and watch them massacred by smallpox!'

'But Vance...'

He didn't have time to argue. He needed to get himself a horse, grab some rations and get on Egan's trail as quickly as possible. Rather than try and explain his feelings to Stormy, and risk being his usual tongue-tied and clumsy self, he whirled about and pulled her into his arms. Without warning, he kissed her flush on the mouth, desperately attempting to express with action what he couldn't put into words.

He pushed away from her a mere moment later and stepped away. Before she could react or slap him for his brashness, he blurted out:

'Don't agree to court or marry anyone

168

until I get back. That's all I ask!'

'Vance!' Stormy was breathless, a shocked expression on her face, 'I ... I...'

There was no time. He threw her a wave and bolted across the compound to the gate. He needed to round up a horse and saddle, then get after Egan. He hadn't told Stormy the whole truth about why he had to stop Egan and Buckley, but it was imperative that those two men should not escape.

Captain Buckley had been waiting for Egan, expecting news of his encounter with Jardeen. He listened as Egan told him what had happened.

'Since you failed to deter him, Jardeen likely suspects you and I are behind the infection of the Indian populace.'

'Not much doubt about it, Cap. I grabbed what supplies were handy and stole Jardeen's horse,' Egan explained. 'I figured we could use him as a pack-animal.'

Buckley looked over the mount and gave a nod of satisfaction. 'Good thinking, Sergeant. I suspect, if we were to return to the fort, we would be placed under arrest.'

Egan was ready to go, but Buckley stopped him with a smile.

'I think I'll try out Mr Jardeen's horse and

169

rig. His appears to be a comfortable riding saddle, and I'm betting he has good taste when it comes to his riding stock.'

'The steed does look durable, Cap,' Egan agreed.

They took a few minutes to load Buckley's animal down with water and supplies and put him on a lead rope.

'What now, Cap?'

'We ride hard and long,' Buckley answered. 'We should have a full day's head start before the colonel can call in his patrols and organize any kind of pursuit.'

'What direction are we going?'

'There's a hundred miles of nothing west of here, no towns, no railroad, no civilization at all. We'll go that way.'

'And then?' Egan wanted to know.

'Mexico, Sergeant. I believe we'll ride down that way and offer our services to General Diaz. The United States is backing him in the revolution down there. It will be the same as fighting for our own government!'

'Yeah, the man is fighting to restore order to Mexico,' Egan replied, thinking along the same lines. 'I'll bet he'll make you an officer right off, Cap. No telling how high you could climb in an army like his.'

Buckley smiled, a light entering his eyes. For so long he had been only seeking his revenge against Yellow Hand. Now he could return to the life he loved. He would again lead men into battle and plan strategy against a fresh enemy. It would be a new lease on life.

'We'll fight together again, my friend, the two of us, side by side.'

'We've no time to lose, Cap,' Egan pointed out. 'If the army catches up with us, we'll likely end up in front of a firing squad.'

'Our job is done here, Sergeant. The foe has been vanquished.'

With those words, Buckley started the horses moving.

Stormy entered town on the borrowed horse. She had thought to try the jail, but spied the man she was looking for coming out of the saddle shop.

'Mr Irish!' she called out, stopping him in his tracks.

Big Irish walked over and a wide grin spread across his face.

'Is it letting you out on a leash for a walk, they are?' he asked. 'Story is, you and Jardeen have been tending to them sick Indians.'

'Mr Jardeen said the two of you were no

longer enemies.'

Irish chuckled. 'Ay, he won me over with a solid right hook.'

'Would you be willing to help him, if he were in desperate trouble?'

The man frowned. 'What is it you're saying? Be the Indian-lover in trouble?'

Stormy quickly explained how Buckley and Egan had intentionally infected the Indians with smallpox, about the attempt on Vance's life, and how he had given chase alone.

'What be that lad of yours thinking?' Irish said with a grunt. 'He hadn't ought to be going after two professional soldiers by himself.'

'He was afraid they would get away.'

'And what would you have me do, lassie?' Irish asked. 'Pray tell, isn't the army going to send men to bring back those two varmints?'

'I'm afraid they will be too late. They have men out on patrols all over the country. By the time they get organized for a chase, Buckley might be as far as Colorado or Utah.'

'So you're asking me to take a couple of me mates and follow on your beau's back trail whilst the army gets organized?'

Stormy could not hide her dread.

'As you said, Mr Irish, those two are professional soldiers. If they decide to stop and fight, Mr Jardeen won't stand a chance. Won't you please help?'

Irish emitted a throaty laugh. 'Ay, lassie. I see how much the Indian-lover means to you. Topper and Jinx be about town. I'll round them up and we'll take a ride.'

Stormy reached out and took his big gnarly hand between her own. 'Oh, thank you, Mr Irish! Thank you!'

He laughed again. 'Not to worry, lassie. Jinx be an ex-army scout himself. If he set his mind to it, he could follow a gnat through a swamp. We'll track down those blokes before them soldier boys can get astride their steeds. Big Irish will bring back your man.'

Stormy told him the direction Jardeen and the two soldiers had taken and thanked him again. Irish assured her they would make all haste and hurried off to find his friends. In a few minutes, the three men were riding out of town at a lope. She waved a last time and returned to her horse. She needed to get back to the Indian camp. Without the corporal and Vance, they were extremely short-handed.

Still, she was glad she had made the effort.

Big Irish seemed sincere and Jinx sounded capable. It would be easier for her to care for the sick, if she knew help was on the way for Vance.

Now if he only waits for them to catch up, she thought.

CHAPTER ELEVEN

The trail left by the three horses was not difficult to follow. Vance didn't know a great deal about the lay of the land, but the country ahead appeared to be vast and empty. Gently rolling hills were visible as far as the eye could see.

Vance had several days of rations. After three days on the trail, he felt he was no closer than when he had started. This chase could continue for weeks, unless he figured a way to catch up and stop the two men. It was imperative he prevent them from reaching any settlements.

Pausing to rest his horse, he assessed the new direction Buckley had chosen. The route was erratic, yet constant in that they continually went either south or west. He wondered where the man was headed. Logically, he was a professional military man. His entire career had been as a soldier. His direction had to have sound reasoning behind it. So what did that mean?

It was doubtful the two men would ride to

Utah and become farmers. Nor was he likely to turn toward Montana and try his hand at herding cattle. Besides which, there were towns and outposts along either route, places where the soldiers might catch or arrest them. That ruled out their continuing to ride west or going up north. To make a circle and return to the east also made no sense. Their own army would be watching for them to the east. They would be hunted men anywhere they went in the territory.

The notion caused a new notion to enter his head. Of course! Buckley was a military man, a man without a country! Where else would he go?

'Mexico!' Vance said aloud. 'It has to be Mexico.'

The reasoning of the plan made perfect sense. Buckley could offer his services to help fight in the revolution. If he chose the winning side, he might be rewarded with a title and either property or a command of his own.

Jardeen suddenly felt better about the pursuit. With a good idea concerning the direction the two were headed, there was less chance he would lose their trail. The real dilemma would surface if he caught up with them. They were trained soldiers and he was a pencil-pushing representative from the War Department. The odds weren't exactly in his favor.

Buckley and Egan had been on the trail for nearly a week when the captain's horse came up with a stone bruise. By noon, the pack-animal was limping badly.

'Looks like we are going to have to make do with only our riding-stock,' Buckley told Egan. 'We keep going and the pack-horse will be ruined.'

'Rotten luck, Cap.'

'We'll leave everything we don't need. I've been using Jardeen's bedding at nights anyway.'

'I meant to ask you about it, Cap,' Egan joked. 'Does he have a feather pillow wrapped up in his ground blanket?'

'No, but he does have a nice warm bedroll. He might be a city slicker from the War Department, but he...'

Egan glanced at Buckley, wondering why he had stopped talking. Instead of asking him outright, he checked the direction in which the man was looking.

'An army patrol?' he asked, trying to see their back trail.

'Too little dust for more than one or two

men,' Buckley replied. 'Have a look with your field glasses.'

Egan dug out a small, collapsible telescope and surveyed the area. When he came to a large dot, he extended the length of the scope to bring the object closer.

'Well, I'll be the son of a third-generation hermit! It's Jardeen!'

Buckley grunted his disgust.

'What was I just saying about him being a city slicker from the War Department?'

'I don't see anyone else.'

'He came after us alone? All by himself?' Buckley was incredulous.

'Looks that way, Cap,' Egan answered. 'He looks to be moving pretty fast. I'd guess he will be on us by dark, maybe earlier than that.'

'And we have a lame horse to boot!'

'What's the plan, Cap?'

Buckley looked off to the trail ahead. They needed to find some decent cover. If they were to stop out in the open, Jardeen would spot them. They had to find a place to set up an ambush.

'I knew we shouldn't have stopped the past couple nights.'

'We needed the sleep and the horses needed the rest, Cap. He must really be pushing his animal to have gained so much ground.'

Buckley snorted. 'Yes, he doesn't have to concern himself about saving his mount's strength. He doesn't plan on it carrying him another thousand miles.'

'What do we do about him?'

Buckley gave it some thought, searching for a plan or idea.

'He's still a long way off,' he said. 'Let's get my horse off-loaded and we'll leave him. We'll take only what we can carry and pick up the pace. If we can reach those distant foothills well ahead of our Indian-loving friend, we can find a place where we can ambush him.'

Egan bobbed his head in agreement.

'With him making such haste to overtake us, he'll ride right into our sights.'

'The man's no fool,' Buckley warned. 'He has managed to stick on our trail for several days.'

'He probably doesn't know we have spotted him, Cap. When he finds we've left our pack-animal, he might really start to push.'

'Yes, and coming so hard, by the time he realizes we've stopped, it'll be too late for him.' Buckley grunted his satisfaction.

'That's the plan, Sergeant. We'll let him come to us and shoot his mount.'

'That will stop him cold.' Egan also chuckled at the thought. 'Unless he is fool enough to keep after us on foot.'

'This is his last chance to live,' Buckley replied to that. 'If he manages to somehow show up again, we'll have to stop him permanently.'

'About the only kind of man who can follow a horse on foot is an Apache warrior, and Jardeen sure ain't no Apache. This idea ought to do it, Cap. We'll strand him like a castaway on an island.'

Buckley took the lead and Egan followed along with the spare horse in tow. They had nothing against Jardeen, but he intended to take them back to be shot or imprisoned. That was motivation to stop the man at any cost – even his life.

Vance was surprised to see the horse. It was nibbling what fodder it could find amongst the sagebrush and an occasional clump of will grass. When it took a step, he understood. The horse had come up lame.

A shiver of anticipation shot through him. With the two men loaded down with supplies, they would not make very good time. He would make a sizable gain on their lead by nightfall.

Kicking his horse into a rapid walk, he took note of the marks on the ground ahead. The horses were moving at a steady, but unhurried pace. He had glimpsed the two men from a rise that morning. They were mere specks in the distance, but he had closed the distance considerably.

His mount was a good one. The gelding had a strong gait and kept a faster pace than most horses. With this new bit of excitement, the sense of urgency was transmitted to the animal. He seemed to know the importance of catching up to their prey.

Several hours passed and, as the sun dipped low on the horizon, Vance expected he might catch a glimpse of the two fugitives at the next rise. He spoke softly to the horse and patted him on the neck for encouragement. He was looking at his mount when he noticed the animal's ears suddenly perk forward. As he had spoken from his back, why would he show an interest in something up ahead?

Vance instinctively ducked low in the saddle. The action came at the very moment he heard the crack of a rifle. His horse buckled and went down. Vance kicked free of the stirrups and rolled from the back of the falling animal.

He hit the ground on his hands and knees, then scurried back to use the horse for cover. The single shot had been deadly, for his horse had died instantly. Vance grabbed hold of the Springfield carbine and yanked it from its scabbard. Then he dug out and shoved a handful of bullets into his pocket. Converted to fire a .45-70 round, it was only a single-shot rifle. He feared the man who had fired at him was using his own Winchester '66. The assailant had a distinct advantage, using a weapon that, fully loaded, held up to sixteen rounds.

A second shot kicked up dirt in front of the dead horse. Vance quickly dived behind a scraggly sagebrush and shoved his rifle out in front of him, ready to fire instantly.

'You should have stuck to tending your redskin pals!' It was Egan. 'You keep trying to follow us and you are going to end up as dead as your horse.'

Vance determined the sergeant's approximate distance and location from the sound of his voice.

'The army will be here in a matter of minutes, Egan. There's no place you can run where they won't catch up to you.'

'That's not much of a bluff, Jardeen,' Egan scoffed. 'I saw Dowd heading for the fort. I know the way the army works. Dowd reported his suspicions to the colonel, then the colonel had to decide a plan of action. After a couple hours of thinking about it, he probably ordered Dowd to send out couriers to call in several of the patrols. It would have taken more than a full day before the colonel could have issued orders for any troops to pursue us.'

Vance began to inch along on his belly, seeking to reach a slight cavity in the trail. If he could move around far enough to get behind Egan, he might be able to surprise him.

'I could have shot you instead of your horse, Jardeen.' Egan spoke up again. 'You keep after us and you'll die out here. Give up your chase. The captain and I only want to leave the country.'

'You infected a whole tribe, Egan,' Vance called, continuing his slow progress. 'You killed nearly a hundred human beings. I can't let you get away with that.'

'It was nothing more than a final act of war, Jardeen. Yellow Hand had it coming. His warriors slaughtered dozens of settlers.'

Vance reached the low spot and lay flat.

With a few weeds about, he was hidden from view. Egan would have to rise up to a standing position to see him. If he did that, he would be exposed to Vance's fire.

'You're out of the race,' Egan baited him again. 'So long as you are on foot, you aren't going to keep up with us.'

Vance remained quiet, his rifle at the ready, cocked, with his finger on the trigger.

Egan was obviously wary of his silence. He stopped the chatter too.

Straining his ears, Vance could detect the man moving. He would be keeping low, with his rifle trained to the spot where Vance had last been. If he should decide to circle wide, he would be able to see the indentation in the ground and Vance would be an easy shot.

Twisting ever so slightly, Vance kept his rifle at his shoulder, watching, holding his breath. If he got any chance at all, it would only be for a split second.

Minutes passed and there was no sound.

Sweat formed on Vance's forehead and a bead slid slowly from his temple to his jaw. His heart was thundering so hard in his chest, he feared Egan would hear it. His breaths were shallow and silent, yet it sounded as though he was wheezing like a wind-broke horse. He tightened his finger on the trigger and watched for any sign of movement.

If Egan was moving, he had the stealth of a cat. Vance continued to listen intently, trying to determine where the man had gone.

After a few minutes, there came the sound of an approaching horse. Vance risked rising up enough to cast a quick glance up the trail. Captain Buckley was approaching. The man had his rifle out and ready to fire. Not knowing where Egan was located, to try and get off a shot was probably to end up dead.

'Sergeant?' Buckley called out. 'Give a shout. Where is he?'

'He's near the trail, Cap!' the man's voice called back. 'About a hundred feet from his downed horse!'

Jardeen groaned his defeat. Egan knew his exact position. These two were professional Indian fighters. It was ridiculous of him to think he could outwit them.

'You are a determined man, Jardeen,' Buckley shouted, 'but you're done. No horse, on foot, with a hundred miles between you and civilization. You're going to need every bit of luck you can manage just to get back in one piece.'

Vance heard the distinct movement of

horses, but he knew one or both men would have their guns trained in his direction. It would have been suicide to try and stop them.

'You should give yourselves up,' Vance called out. 'You're going to be wanted men for the rest of your lives.'

The captain chuckled.

'Only in this country, Jardeen,' he replied back. 'You've lost this engagement. Don't lose your life as well.'

Vance anchored his teeth, angered by how easily they had stopped him. He had not been prepared for the two men to stop and fight. He should have known they would do just that, once they spied him on their back trail. He should have been ready.

He heard the sound of horses leaving the area and at last risked a peek over the tall grass. Buckley and Egan were making haste to get out of rifle range.

Vance stood up and stared after the two men. To fire off a round or two would have been wasted effort, especially with only the single-shot carbine. He probably couldn't have hit them in a hundred tries at that distance.

Jardeen considered giving chase on foot. It wasn't long before nightfall. If they didn't expect him to follow, they might stop in two or three hours – possibly ten or fifteen miles. If he walked all night, he might reach them by morning.

He dismissed the idea as foolhardy. They had proved they were professionals. They would choose a place they could defend and keep watch. If he managed to catch up with them, he would likely only get himself killed.

Returning to his fallen mount, he patted the lifeless animal.

'I'm sorry, boy,' he murmured softly. 'You gave me your best and I got you killed for your efforts. That's another debt I owe those two.'

Stripping off what gear he could carry, he decided his only option was to start back to civilization. He had a full canteen, along with some jerky and hard rolls. It would be a long trek, but, if he managed thirty miles a day, he ought to reach a settlement in three days.

With a final sigh of defeat, he slung his canteen over his shoulder, tucked his bedroll under his arm and picked up his carbine. Then he began to walk.

Egan found a hollow, between several small hills, where he could use some dried wood to make a smokeless fire. Once he had heated coffee and beans, he let the embers die and buried them with a thick layer of dirt. The chance that anyone would have seen the fire was remote and there had been very little smoke for anyone to smell. He was pretty sure they were safe.

'Chow and coffee's ready, Cap,' he called softly.

Buckley had been sitting just below the summit of the knoll, where he could watch and listen to the night.

'Nothing moving out there,' Buckley told him, walking over to fill a cup of hot coffee and take a tin plate of beans. 'We'll take turns keeping watch all the same.'

'Jardeen?'

'We've come a good fifteen miles since we left him. He shouldn't follow, but he proved he was a determined man. If he were to follow us on foot, he might get lucky.'

'*Unlucky* is more like it, Cap,' Egan said. 'If he comes after us again, we'll stop him for good.'

'Yes, and that would be a shame. He seems a good man.'

The two of them ate in silence. Then Egan picked up his rifle to take the first watch. Buckley spread out his poncho and blankets and stretched out on the ground.

'I'll tell you one thing,' Buckley said to Egan. 'Jardeen has himself a nice warm blanket in his bedroll. I knew he would be the kind to pamper himself like a girl.'

'He might be a sissy about some things, Cap,' Egan replied back, 'but he didn't fight like a girl. He whipped Big Irish, and him still suffering from being dragged behind a horse. Then the man comes after us all alone. He has some grit, that one.'

'You're right about that, Sergeant. I don't blame a man for enjoying his comfort.' Then came a chuckle, 'Especially when I'm the one who has been enjoying his pampering these last few nights.'

'Good night, Cap,' Egan called, as he headed up the nearby hill.

'Wake me at midnight,' Buckley answered back. 'I'll stand watch till dawn and we'll get an early start.'

Egan climbed the knoll and stopped a few feet from the peak. Even in the darkness, he knew better than to expose himself along the top of the hill. A hunter with good night vision might pick out the uneven silhouette of a man framed against a dark moonlit sky. By staying lower than the horizon, he could keep watch without exposing an outline.

189

Sitting quietly, he studied the sounds of the night. There was total silence, except for a cricket off in the distance. Someone once told him a person could tell the temperature by counting the number of times a cricket chirped in a minute. He had never given the notion much credence, but there were some strange things in the world. He supposed it could be true.

However, nothing seemed more strange than to have a city slicker like Jardeen risking his life to catch them. He had come to Wyoming to count and log the Indians for transfer to a reservation. He should have had no personal interest in them. They were nothing to him. He had not been around to fight the battles or wars with them. He had never seen the slaughter of a pilgrim wagon train or visited a burned-out settlement after they were finished. He didn't know the terror of being surrounded by a bunch of bloodthirsty Indians, trembling with fear for his family and his own life.

No, Jardeen was from the War Department, where they still endorsed an insane logic about being able to make peace and live together with the Indians. How could that come about, when the Indians refused to give up their nomadic, carefree way of

190

life. The men liked the freedom of moving from place to place, where the only work involved was hunting and fishing. For as long as there had been different clans, they had gone on raids and done battle with neighboring tribes each spring. It was sport, part of the fun of being a warrior.

Meanwhile, the poor Indian women worked constantly. They set up the camp and watched the children, while they tended the fires, cooked and chewed the fat from animal hides to make moccasins or clothes. Had the army waged war against abused, work-laden Indian women, it would have been a short war indeed. They would have welcomed a change of life with open arms.

Egan shook his head. Such things were the fodder for politicians and men of foresight. All throughout the history of the world, people had fought wars and conquered each other. The battle against the Indians was no different from the aftermath of the Civil War, he decided. Change was constant in the universe and the only way to survive was to change with the times.

A smile curled his lips. The captain would surely laugh to know he was indulging in such deep thoughts. They had ridden together for a decade and never had he shared philosophical perspectives with the captain. It wasn't necessary, as Buckley did the thinking for them both. He never failed to listen to Egan's advice, but he had always been the man in charge. Both of them liked it that way.

Egan spent a cool evening and eventually rolled and lit a cigarette. It was something usually forbidden while on guard duty, as an enemy could see the glowing tip of a cigarette from a hundred yards away. However, unless Jardeen had run most of the way, he wouldn't be able to catch up with them before daylight. Such was his reasoning for risking a smoke.

Midnight arrived without incident and Egan trudged back to camp. He would have let the captain rest a bit longer, but Buckley was adamant about his orders. Rather than have him angered that he had let him sleep past the appointed hour, he knew to wake him on schedule.

'Cap?' he said softly, approaching the man's bedroll. 'It's time, Cap.'

Buckley was instantly awake.

'Midnight already?' he said, sitting up. 'It feels like I just closed my eyes.'

'Time does pass more quickly sleeping than sitting on a rock,' Egan agreed. 'Instead of rolling out my own blankets, I thought maybe I would use your...'

When he stopped in mid-sentence, Buckley frowned up at him. 'What?'

'That blanket!' Egan cried, pointing at the cover Buckley had been using. 'You've been sleeping in *that* blanket since we left Camp Sage?'

Buckley displayed confusion at Egan's sharp tone.

'What about it, Sergeant?'

Egan dropped to his knees and took hold of the quilt. He felt the ruffled edge and checked the pattern. There could be no doubt of its origin.

'I didn't know, Cap,' he muttered gravely. 'We've been going to bed well after dark and I didn't see it before.'

'What the blazes are you talking about, Egan? Stop mumbling!'

'The quilt – it's from the Indian camp, Cap!' He shook his head from side to side. 'I took it from the wagon train, along with a few others. It's one of those I gave to the Indians to spread the smallpox.'

Buckley came out of the bed as though a snake had suddenly slithered between his ankles.

'What?' he cried. 'Are you sure?'

'Can't be two blankets like that around. Jardeen and Dowd must have been going to use it as evidence against us. I'll bet the Indian-lover was going to wash it first, then present it to the colonel as evidence.'

'Maybe Jardeen had already washed it.' Buckley suggested, his face blanched with fear. 'Maybe he cleaned it first.'

'He didn't have time,' Egan replied. 'He was getting ready to leave when I stole his mount. There's no way it was ever at the cleansing station.' He could not hide the dire foreboding which invaded his very being. 'It's straight from the Indian camp, Cap.'

Buckley was on his feet and pacing now.

'I've slept in that bed ever since we left the Fort.'

'You can use what water we have, Cap,' Egan was quick to offer. 'Toss your clothes and strip down. We'll wash and scrub you until there ain't a single germ left on your body.'

Buckley started to unbutton his shirt, but stopped.

'It's a little late for precautions now, Sergeant. If I've been contaminated, I've been contaminated.'

Egan suffered with the weight of the truth as well. The captain had been sleeping in the quilt for several nights. He was right. No amount of washing would help. Buckley had already been exposed to smallpox!

CHAPTER TWELVE

It was mid-morning when Vance spied two riders and three horses. Drawing closer, he was shocked to discover it was Big Irish and Jinx!

'What did I be telling you?' Irish joked to Jinx, as they approached within ear-shot. 'We made the trip for nothing. The lad has everything well in hand.'

'Got himself afoot a hundred miles from the nearest settlement,' Jinx agreed, showing a wide grin. 'Yep, he done just fine on his own.'

'What are you two doing way out here, over a hundred miles from Wayward?' asked Vance.

'They be a fair young lass who has a keen interest in your welfare, mate,' Irish replied. 'We could ill-abide the shedding of tears and lamentful wailing, so we agreed to come and look for you.'

'We're a day behind Egan and Buckley,' Vance apprised them. 'They laid ambush and shot my horse yesterday. However, their pack-animal came up lame, so they aren't going to be traveling very fast.'

'We'll redistribute our supplies and you can ride our pack-horse,' Jinx suggested. 'If we leave everything we don't need behind, we might still overtake them boys before they leave the territory.'

It was the eleventh day of tracking the two deserters when Jinx paused to look at a dark blotch which stained the earth. 'Looks like someone lost his breakfast,' he observed. 'Maybe one of the soldier boys is sick.'

'It's smallpox,' Jardeen told them both. 'It's the reason I've been so desperate to catch them, before they could reach a settlement. We can't let them spread the disease.'

'Say, howdy!' Jinx swore vehemently. 'No one said anything about the plague!'

'If we get close enough to take them, I'll be the only one who makes any physical contact. Egan and I have both had the disease, so we can't get it again.'

'Ay, sounds good enough for you, mate,' Irish complained. 'But Jinx and myself won't be a-going along. We be smart enough to stay shed of that pestilence.'

'You need only help me catch up with them – I'll do the rest.'

'You say so, do you?' Irish was not convinced. 'And how about taking them boys back for trial? Will you be doing that alone too?'

'Yes, so long as there is any chance of spreading smallpox. I don't want either of you getting too close.'

'We've been close to you already!'

'I took all of the necessary precautions when I left the camp. My horse and I were clean. Buckley has gotten himself infected from a blanket I was going to use as evidence against him.'

'I smell ambush,' Jinx said, stopping their progress. 'The trail goes between those two hills up ahead. If Buckley is getting sick, they have to try and stop us now, before he gets too sick to fight.'

Jardeen scanned the area up ahead. There was adequate brush for hiding to each side of the hollow. Jinx was probably right.

'How do we approach?' he asked.

'On foot, one to each side and one down the middle.'

'The one going up the middle will be a sitting duck,' Jardeen pointed out.

'It's your party,' Jinx told him. 'I reckon that makes you the volunteer target.'

'Jinx and me will move out first,' Irish suggested. 'You give us time to work our way around them hills. Once we get in position, we should be ready for anyone who tries to shoot at you.'

'That's very reassuring.'

'We are willing to listen if you have a better plan, mate?'

Jardeen shook his head and the two men dropped to the ground. Each tied off his horse, took his rifle and began to skirt the brush. Keeping low, they moved toward the dangerous-looking ravine.

Egan held his rifle ready, but the three riders stopped at the entrance to the small pass. Once he saw Jinx was leading the trio, he felt his hopes dashed. Jinx was no fool. The man had been a good scout and knew the ear-marks of a trap.

Rather than hold his position, he moved from the hill and hurried to make his way back to Captain Buckley. He experienced an emptiness in his chest at seeing his longtime commander and friend.

Buckley was not lying in wait for the approaching riders. He was sprawled on his back, his face a mask of agony, struck hard by the cramps and fever. The redness about his face had developed a host of pimples which would soon fill with pus. Then would come delirium and loss of control over his digestive system. He would become dehydrated and be out of his head. The fever would rake his body and the pustules would cover his body. He would be no help in the coming fight.

Egan picked up the canteen and attempted to force a few drops down Buckley's throat. It caused him to choke and he coughed it right back up. There was blood in his spittle. The smallpox had a strong grip on him. If he was to live, he would need a lot of care.

Egan made his decision and took up a position where he could protect the captain. The only chance for escape was for him to kill all three of the men who were following. That would allow him to care for Buckley and see him through to recovery. If they were captured, the plague would not be their only concern, for a life in prison awaited them both.

Egan heard someone going through the brush. He whirled about and fired!

The shot startled a small buck, a young one with only nubs for antlers. The deer bounded away over the hill and was quickly out of sight.

'The shot came from up near the summit of the hill on the north!' Jinx called to Vance and Big Irish. 'I don't see the other one.'

'He's probably down sick!' Vance called back. 'Once a person starts to heave from smallpox, it's only a short while till he's down with fever.'

Irish appeared on the side of the northern hill and waved. He pointed to his intended route, which would take him around the hill. He would circle back and come in from above.

Jinx was where he could see the man signalling. He motioned to Vance that he would work the other side, gaining the high ground, where he could be even with or above the shooter.

Vance took the frontal position and began to make some progress up the hill. He would make a direct approach, then try and talk sense into Egan. At least, he had been thinking on those lines.

A bullet chipped rock not a foot from his head. As the shot echoed down the hill, Vance dived for cover. He snuggled up next to a cozy rock and kept his head down.

'Give it up, Egan!' he called. 'You can't win against three of us.'

'The captain ain't going back to stand trial

– not for killing a bunch of red-hide butchers who slaughtered his wife and child!'

'I'm sure they will take that into consideration at his hearing,' Vance replied.

'Yeah, they'll listen and offer their sympathy – right before they send us both to prison for the rest of our lives.'

'You killed a hundred old people and women and children, Egan. There isn't any defense for a crime like that.'

Egan fired another round. It went high and wide.

Vance remained hidden and protected. He was not in any position to shoot up the hill. He didn't have to. Irish and Jinx would soon reach a place where they could offer return fire.

'I know the captain is down sick, Sergeant.' Vance tried to reason with Egan. 'If you and I tend to him together, we might save him.'

'The captain isn't going to die in some stinking prison.'

'Use your head, Sergeant,' Vance called out again. 'There are three of us against just you and an army patrol several hours back of us. This is a fight you can't win.'

There was a long silence, but his bluff about a patrol that might or might not be coming caused the man to ponder his limited options. Eventually Egan replied in a calm, level voice.

'You're right, Jardeen. The fighting is over.'

Even as Vance wondered what that meant he heard a shot. His instinct was to duck lower, but the bullet had not been aimed at him. A moment passed and there came a second shot.

Vance slowly stood up. He had his rifle, but it was not ready for use. He knew what had happened.

'They're both down!' Irish shouted to him. 'Egan … he shot the captain and then turned the gun on himself!'

'Don't get near the bodies,' Vance called back. 'I'll see to them.'

'You'll not be having to tell Jinx nor I to stay shed of them two,' Irish responded. 'The burial detail be all yours.'

Three weeks had passed since Vance had set out after Captain Buckley and Sergeant Egan. Vance shook hands and parted company with Jinx and Big Irish at the entrance to Wayward. Then he rode in and reined up his horse at the front of the laundry. It was about quitting time for Stormy. If Corporal

Dowd or someone else wasn't waiting for her, he hoped he might...

'Vance!' a frantic voice cried. 'Vance! Is it you?'

He climbed down in time to get nearly knocked over by a low-flying body! Stormy ran into his arms and embraced him tightly, clinging to him.

'I was so afraid for you!' she sobbed against his shoulder. 'I thought you might have been killed.'

'Took me a while to catch up with the captain. If you hadn't sent Irish and Jinx to help, I would never have gotten the job done.'

'Buckley and Egan were trained soldiers.' She scolded him with her tone of voice. 'You had no right going after them alone!'

'There wasn't time for anything else. They were carrying an infected blanket and almost made their escape. I couldn't risk another outbreak from smallpox.'

'But you got them?' Stormy asked.

'They are both dead and buried. Everything they had with them was tossed into a fire pit.'

Stormy recovered her aplomb and looked at him, dusty from travel, unshaven, with sweat-stained clothes.

'And what will you do now?' she asked.

Vance carefully placed his hands to either side of her face, gently tilted her head back and kissed her soundly.

'I'd like to take you away from this sweat factory,' Vance said, leaning back to study her beautiful features. 'I'd be right happy if you would consent to marry me.'

Stormy's eyes misted, while she smiled demurely.

'You've never even asked to court me proper.'

'Maybe not, but we've spent our share of time together.'

'It's been mostly misery, Vance. I do hope you have something else in mind for our future?'

'Nothing but a home and children and happiness, little darlin'!'

'And where would we live?' she asked. 'I'm not going to run about the country seeing to the settlement of Indians.'

'Once I see to the disposition of Yellow Hand's people, I'm going to accept an office position in Denver. I think it's time to settle down in one place.'

'I like that idea,' Stormy purred, leaning close to kiss Vance a second time. 'Yes, I like that idea a lot.'

Vance held her close and said a quiet prayer of thanks. The heartbreak, the misery and Captain Buckley's final vengeance were behind them. It was time to start fresh, to share their lives together.

That had a wonderful ring to it ... a very nice ring indeed!

The publishers hope that this book has given you enjoyable reading. Large Print Books are especially designed to be as easy to see and hold as possible. If you wish a complete list of our books please ask at your local library or write directly to:

Dales Large Print Books
Magna House, Long Preston,
Skipton, North Yorkshire.
BD23 4ND

This Large Print Book, for people
who cannot read normal print,
is published under the auspices of

THE ULVERSCROFT FOUNDATION